Moments
The Story of Gil and Macey

DWIGHT JONES

MOMENTS-THE STORY OF GIL AND MACEY

Copyright © 2018 Dwight Jones

All rights reserved.

ISBN: 9781790872183

ISBN-13:

DEDICATION

To my wonderful wife, Tammy Jones, and to my Daughters,
Heather, Candace and Chelsea. I love you all more than words
could ever tell. Thank you to each of you for your love and
support and for making life's MOMENTS so memorable

MOMENTS-THE STORY OF GIL AND MACEY

CHAPTERS

1	GILBERT OLIVER THOMPSON	1
2	THE DEATH OF A HERO	7
3	217 WILLOW STREET	12
4	SOMETHING GOT AHOLD' OF GIL	21
5	HAZEL AND IRENE	27
6	IRENE AND ROBERT	31
7	MATTHEW THOMPSON	40
8	A NEW HOME IN SALYERSVILLE?	51
9	THE MEETING	71
10	DINNER WITH THE PREACHER	76
11	THE DATE	82
12	INNOCENCE LOST	87
13	THE LONG AWAITED TALK	91

CHAPTERS

14	A NEW ASSIGNMENT	99
15	RUNNING OUT OF LUCK	104
16	SISTER IRENE	118
17	FROM BAD TO WORSE	123
18	A COLD NIGHT IN DECEMBER	131
19	AN INVITATION HE COULDN'T REFUSE	141
20	ANOTHER CHANCE	155
21	COMING TO GRIPS	167
22	NO MORE CHURCH TALK	174
23	STOP-DEATH-STOP	182
24	BAD TIMING	187

MOMENTS-THE STORY OF GIL AND MACEY

ACKNOWLEDGMENTS

I WOULD LIKE TO SAY THANK YOU TO MY MOM AND DAD FOR ALL THAT THEY ENDURED WHILE RAISING SEVEN BOYS AND A GIRL DURING SOME DIFFICULT YEARS. WHILE THERE WERE MANY HARD TIMES ALONG THE WAY, MUCH OF WHAT I AM TODAY IS OWED TO THOSE MOMENTS AT THE HOUSE ON HIGHWAY N AND ON JJ IN IRON COUNTY. MORE THAN ANYTHING THAT SERVED TO DEFINE ME, IT WAS THE GRACE OF GOD AND HIS LIFE CHANGING POWER THAT BROKE THE CURSE OF SIN AND DEATH OFF OF MY LIFE.

MOMENTS-THE STORY OF GIL AND MACEY

CHAPTER 1

GILBERT OLIVER THOMPSON

He had been a formidable man, back in the day. His brown wavy hair had turned gray, and although he was still more than six foot tall, his stature had diminished as the years had passed. He now showed the signs of a man who had seen more than his share of heartaches and hardships. His deep brown eyes had lost a little of the sparkle that had once been there and laugh lines had been replaced by deep wrinkles along the way. Back in high school, Gil stood six foot two inches tall, but everyone thought he was much taller than that. He had been the star quarterback and a pretty good point guard in the local high school. Many of the boys who played basketball and football at Purdin were arrogant and boastful, and although some of them were decent athletes, not all of them excelled in the classroom.

Gil, on the other hand was a strong student as well. Actually it was his studies that he enjoyed most and he was a natural. He was humble and kind, there was never a proud strut around campus, and unless you watched him play football on Friday nights or drain the net with an outside shot, that always looked perfect, you would never have known what kind of athlete he was.

He had been raised in a different hour. He was taught that it mattered more what you thought of yourself than what other people said about you. He was not self-absorbed or conceited, honestly he was quite the opposite. The standard that Gil had for himself was so high; it seemed at times to be unattainable. It was a trait that he had learned early in life not from his dad, but from his grandfather.

Gil's father had never been a part of his life. It used to bother him a lot, but his grandpa Oliver seemed to fill that void. It was he who showed Gilbert "how to carry himself," as grandpa used to put it. It was more than a matter of walking with confidence and having a quiet demeanor, there was just something about "knowing who you are on the inside and once you get that figured out, all of the other stuff takes care of itself." He could still hear grandpa Gil saying those words to him as they were walking through the woods. Ostensibly they were on a squirrel hunting expedition, but Gil knew that anytime he went somewhere with grandpa Ollie, he was going to school. Oliver would teach on matters of great importance, like how to skin a squirrel or sometimes he would use an old colloquialism such as, "fishins' best when the winds from the west." Oh there were times when the conversation was deep and grandpa would explain to him, "the real value of a man is not what other's say about you, it is what you, know about yourself."

The lessons that Gil learned from Grandpa Oliver were invaluable. It was one of those lessons that would ultimately change Gil. One day after school he grabbed his pole and ran to the pond to 'wet the hook,' as Grandpa Ollie would say. The fish weren't biting, but somehow that didn't seemed to matter much to either Gil or his grandpa. They just sat there watching the cork bounce up and down with the gentle breeze that was blowing across the old pond on the back of the farm. Gil sat on the stump of an old willow tree, a tree he was glad to see gone. He remembered when he was little, every time that he would cast his rod, he would tangle his line up in one of its limbs.

Gil sat there listening to his grandpa whistle a tune and watching both of their lines move with the breeze, he asked, "Grandpa, why did you cut this old willow down?" Ollie quit whistling and just chuckled, "Well son, I really had no choice. Most of the limbs were torn out of it because of all of the fishhooks that ended up in them. The ones that were left were so thick with fishing line that I was afraid someone might get hanged in them or a bird might get tangled up in the line." Gilbert laughed at the thought of someone hanging in a fishing line. It was true; he couldn't remember a time that he had gone fishing at the pond without getting tangled up in that tree.

When he had stopped laughing, Gil asked grandpa Ollie another question, but this one wasn't quite so light and the response was not so jovial. "Grandpa.' Gil said, 'What ever happened to my dad? How come he never came to see me?" Ollie wished the question hadn't come up but, it did and he sat there for a moment trying to figure out how exactly he was going to answer it. "Well, that's a tough question son." Ollie continued. "I guess it's kind of like the old willow that use to be here, the longer it hung around, the more problems there would have been for you. You would have spent your whole life trying to untangle your line from one of its branches." "What do you mean?" Gil asked. "Well son, what I am trying to say is, your dad was a lot like this old willow, he had a way of creating messes everywhere he went.

Just like those old fishing lines, hanging down from the limbs of this tree served as a reminder of a bad cast, your dad seemed to leave lines hanging. Everywhere he went he left broken limbs and broken lines and too many times he left broken hearts also. You see, son, the hardest part of life is having to make decisions that are hurtful for the moment, but over time have a way of saving us from even more pain." Oliver was trying to be vague enough to keep from hurting his grandson but straight enough that perhaps Gilbert would understand the not-so-subtle message. It must have worked because Gil just nodded as though he had fully grasped what his grandpa was saying. Ollie breathed a sigh of relief and again looked toward the bobber floating there on the water when Gil spoke up. "Grandpa, thank you for cutting down that old willow, it makes a better stump than it did a shade tree anyway."

Ollie started to respond but just then he saw Gil's cork go under the water. Before he could say anything he watched Gil pull up on the pole, and with a hard jerk he set the hook. The fight was on; this was going to be one for the records, if his grandson could get him to the bank. Ollie knew there were some 'lunkers' in there, but until now no one seemed to be able to get them to bite. He was giving it all that he had, he would pull and reel, pull and reel and then he just took off running up the bank. The line was stretched tight but it held, and before you know it, skipping up out of the water was one of the biggest bass Oliver had ever seen caught. "Whoa, wait a minute son, your gonna skin him before we get a chance to fillet him." Gilbert threw down the pole and jumped right on top of the bass. Oliver nearly doubled over at the sight of this poor bass under the weight of Gil who had sprawled over it like someone trying to catch a greased pig at the county fair. When Gil got up he was grinning from ear to ear and was shouting to the top of his lungs! "Woo hoo grandpa! It's the biggest fish ever!" It was indeed a big one but not near as big as joy that emanated from Gilbert! Normally Ollie would throw back all of the bass caught but not this one; he was a whopper and was definitely a keeper. There would be no more fish caught that day, Oliver knew that he would never be able to get his grandson to come back to earth let alone do any more fishing. It was just as good, that fish had taken Gilberts mind a million miles from the conversation about Matthew Thompson.

There was something almost mystical about the way his grandpa could make him feel. He was the only grandson, but it wouldn't have mattered if there had been a thousand, because grandpa Oliver just had that ability to make everyone feel like they were the most important person in the world. That was the one thing that people now said about Gil. They would say, "Ole Gil sure has a way of making you feel like you matter doesn't he?" It had been that way when he was in school, which is why everyone looked up to him. Some of his best friends were the poorest or dirtiest kids in school and yet their poverty didn't define him nor did his friendship with the wealthiest students. He was Gil and what he knew about himself was this, he was the luckiest kid in the world because he was the grandson of Mr. Oliver Gilbert Trommel. He always told himself, "If I can be half the man that my grandpa is, I'll be a mighty big man." At times he seemed to live his life looking through the lens of grandpa Ollie's glasses. It was as though he had spent so much time with him that he would weigh every action out and make every decision with the wisdom of that man who was in so many ways, bigger than life. It turned out to be a pretty good way to live and it certainly had saved him a lot of heartache along the way.

"Never quit learning Gil." His grandpa would say. "If you make a mistake, be man enough to admit it, and if you do something that turns out good, chalk it up to the goodness of God." Certainly God had been good to him and even though life had been difficult at times, everything had turned out pretty well.

CHAPTER 2

THE DEATH OF A HERO

The seventh of June was a day Gil would never forget. He had just graduated high school and was looking forward to his last summer with grandpa Ollie before he would move away to college. It was going to be an incredible summer for sure. Him and Ollie had planned to spend the whole summer doing tours of all of their favorite fishing holes. Ollie's eyes would light up and a smile would cover his face every time he would talk about it. All of that changed when Gil was awakened to the sound of his mom crying.

It was barely four o'clock in the morning when he heard her sobbing. Gil rolled out of bed and hurried as fast as he could to his mom's aid. She was sitting on the side of her bed, crying uncontrollably. "What's wrong momma?" He asked. Yet somehow he knew, he knew that the man he loved so much, the man who was his hero, was gone. Gil never heard her response, he sat down by her on the edge of the bed, put his arms around his mother and they wept together.

After a while he asked her what had happened? "They think it was a heart attack honey." She replied. "But, but grandpa never had a bad heart. He was perfectly well yesterday. I helped him load those boards onto his truck yesterday evening because he told me he had pulled a muscle in his arm, but other than that he was fine." Gil said. Hazel explained to him that his "arm cramps, and indigestion issues" as he had called them, were actually symptoms of a very serious heart problem.

"When did it happen Mom, where is grandpa?" Asked Gil. "They found him in his office at work. He told me had a lot of work to get done, so when he didn't come home, I never thought anything of it and just went to bed. When I heard the knock at the door around 3:30 I knew something was wrong." She answered.

The days that followed were hard and a fog had enveloped Gil. By the end of the month, his head was beginning to clear. The reality of not getting to spend the summer with his grandpa is what caused him to take the summer job at the market, besides, making some extra money seemed like a pretty good idea.

Grandpa Oliver had left his family in good shape and for the first time that Gil could remember, his mother did not have to work two jobs to provide. Hazel discovered that work had helped her to keep her mind off of the loss of her daddy. In his last will and testament, grandpa Ollie made certain that his daughters, Hazel and Irene, had been provided for, but it was Gil who was the primary beneficiary. He was the only grandson, so he was given all of the "man stuff" as his cousin's like to refer to it. The gift which he prized the most was Oliver's old pickup truck and of course, his hunting dog.

The fact that he had transportation was the reason he was given the job at Mickelson's. He would be able to use it to deliver groceries.

He had taken the job because he needed a distraction. Gil knew he would never be able to make it through the days ahead with nothing to do. Little did he know that when he got to work at Mickelson's Market, that it would be a day that would change his life.

Eastern Kentucky was experiencing one of the hottest summers that Gil could recall. Although it was only June 28th, it was unusually hot. There was absolutely no breeze blowing, Gil had the wing glass open on the old truck as well as the vent, but it wasn't much help. Usually he loved to listen to the birds and he enjoyed feeling the wind blow through the truck, but the air that came through the truck was like the blast of a furnace, it brought him no relief from the stifling heat. It was miserable!

Some days there weren't many deliveries and he would be able to work in the store, but today wasn't one of those days. It was one delivery after another, all day long. Finally Mr. Mickelson handed him the final delivery address and helped him load the groceries into the passenger seat of the truck. This was going to be his last delivery for the day. Gil was taking off early to take grandpa's dog out and let him run through the woods for a while. Ole Rex just wanted to lie around and whine. "He missed Ollie as much as anyone," Gil surmised. "It will do the ole feller some good to run off some energy," he thought.

Gil had told his mom that he and Rex were going to spend some time together after work and not to wait for him to get home to eat. She smiled and told him to be careful and that she would see him that evening. As he turned to leave, Hazel pulled him to her side and gave him a kiss on the cheek and told him, "Gilbert Oliver Thompson, don't you be out late tonight." Gil smiled and said that he would be careful and would see her later.

As he turned toward the door he thought of the way she called him by his whole name. She was the only one that called him Gilbert; he supposed it was because he was named after her daddy. He didn't mind, actually, he wore the name like a badge of honor. At times he had wished that he had been given the full name of his grandpa and a year earlier, even asked his mom if she would help him get his name changed to Gilbert Oliver Trommel. He didn't know why, but for some reason it just never happened. He would have to live the rest of his life being called by the last name of a dad that he never knew. He would have to make the best of just being Gilbert Oliver Thompson. Gil had never known Matthew Thompson, he often regretted having to bear the name of a man who didn't care enough about him to come and see. But as long as he had Grandpa Ollie, Matthew Thompson didn't really matter, but now he was gone too, Ollie thought as he shifted the truck into first and began to ease out of

MOMENTS-THE STORY OF GIL AND MACEY

the driveway.

CHAPTER 3

217 WILLOW STREET

Gilbert hadn't dated anyone in school, there never seemed to be anyone that struck his fancy. He had never met anyone who even slightly drew his attention, that is, until that particular day. Grandpa Ollie used to tell him, "When you meet the right girl, she will take your breath away." Although nothing like that had ever happened to him, all of that was about to change.

Gil hadn't planned to work as long as he had. He had every intention to drop some things back by Mickelson's and hurry to get Rex for their afternoon run. Between the heat and humidity and the occasional grumpy customer, he couldn't wait to get out in the woods. Mr. Mickelson stopped him as he walked through the back door, "Gilbert, I have one more delivery for you. Now don't worry, it's just a small order." He helped him load the few bags into his truck and gave him the address. "Now these go to 217 Willow Street Gil. You need to hurry because they have to leave. You need to be there by three." Gilbert looked up at the clock and realized it was already 2:47 pm.

He drove as quickly as he possibly could and pulled up in front of 217 Willow at 3:00 on the nose. As he stepped out of the delivery truck and gathered the order up in his arms and turned toward the house,

Gil froze in his tracks.

Standing there by the gate was the most amazing sight he'd ever seen. He instantly began to sweat profusely, Gil tried to act normal, but the more he tried the more strange he felt.

"Hi, I have an order for 712, I mean 217 Willow. Is this the right house?" He was fumbling for words and trying to pull himself together, but it wasn't working so well. The calm quiet demeanor that had always seemed to define him had taken flight.

A head of cabbage rolled out of his arms and onto the sidewalk in front of him. As he bent to pick it up, apologizing profusely and feeling like a total fool, he proceeded to drop more groceries. "Could this get any worse?" he thought. After gathering the groceries and trying to gather his emotions, he looked up, half expecting this beautiful girl to be laughing at him, but to his amazement she wasn't. Instead of mockery or laughter, he was greeted with the most pleasant smile he had ever seen. She reached her hand out to introduce herself and to help him up. Then it dawned on her that he would never be there able to shake her hand or receive her help, not without dropping everything again. Gil stood up, both hands full of groceries and tried to pull himself together. He wanted to take her hand and introduce himself, but he knew better than try that. He felt foolish enough already. "Hi, is this 217 Willow?" He asked again. He was certain that she had already answered him, but she smiled and told him he was at the right address.

She smiled politely and said, "Hello my name is Macey, would you like for me to take one of those bags?" Gil just stood there. She had done to him exactly what Grandpa Oliver said, "She took his breath away." He thought her to be about 5'5" tall; she had the most beautiful blue eyes he had ever seen and long brown hair. He was mesmerized and all he could do was stare. His mouth gaped open; he was totally unable to respond for what seemed like an hour, although it was surely only a few moments. Gone were the confidence, the strength, and the boldness he had always had?

Then he heard her repeat herself, "Would you like me to take one of those bags? With that he was awakened from what seemed to be an eternity of just staring at her. "Oh I am so sorry ma'am! Please forgive me. My name is Gilbert but please call me Gil," he added. After a few more attempts at sounding and acting normal Gil carried the groceries to the door where a man who he assumed to be Macey's father met him. He handed the bags to the gentleman and thanked him for the order, and apologized for the millionth time for having dropped the groceries. He offered to pay for anything that had been damaged and then turned to leave.

He again introduced himself to Macey, as though she hadn't heard him the first time. Now, it was he who had stretched out his hand to shake hers and again apologize for being so careless. Macey shook his hand and smiled at him. When she did, it seemed that the entire world stopped.

Standing there on the sidewalk in front of 217 Willow shaking the hand of the most beautiful girl he had ever seen, Gil finally came to himself. How long had he been holding on to her hand? He had been so engrossed in her beauty that he had lost track of everything else. There wasn't much conversation, but there seemed to be a lot said. Gil excused himself and told her how pleased he was to have met her and made his way back to the truck.

Gil didn't know if this was the "right girl," but he knew one thing for sure, when he saw her he was unable to think clearly. His mind was turned to mush and he found himself unable to formulate words. "What in the world?" He asked himself later. What just happened?

The next few hours Gil was in a daze. He drove to the house and picked up Rex, his plan to let the dog run off some energy, quickly turned into a chance for Gil to think. Gilbert pulled off on the log road that went along the backside of the Johnson farm. These were woods that he and Rex knew well. This had always been Grandpa Ollie's favorite squirrel hunting place. Gil opened the door to get out and was hardly out of the door when Rex shot past him. He bounded out of the truck and was running through the woods barking and chasing everything that moved. Gil seemed to just float along, not even sure if his feet had ever touched the ground.

He replayed the scene at Macey's house, each time trying harder and harder to not seem like a buffoon. Gil scolded himself over and over for dropping the groceries and looking so goofy. "What was I thinking?" He said aloud. "She probably thinks I'm weird!" "Hi, my name is doofy!" He said, making fun of how he responded to Macey.

The sun was beginning to set when he and Rex finally got back to the truck and headed toward home. Even though his house was on the other side of town, Gil decided to drive down Willow Street. He couldn't resist, he had to see if by some twist of fate, Macey might be outside on the porch when he went by. The thought of looking foolish had crossed his mind, but she must already think that, especially after him dropping the groceries. "What if she was outside?" Gil said. Rex looked over at Gil, as though he had been speaking to him.

As he drove by he slowed the truck and tried to look straight ahead but he couldn't keep from stealing a glance in the direction of the house, hoping to see her. Unfortunately there was no one in the yard and it didn't look like anyone was home. Who was this girl? He tried not to stare toward the house, but he couldn't resist.

There was something magnetic about her and he felt it pulling him. Just then it dawned on him, "I don't even know her last name!" He almost yelled it out. Again he said it, but this time in total disbelief, "I don't even know her last name!" Had she told him?

Was he so caught up in the moment that he didn't hear her? How could he have missed such an important piece of information? Either he never heard her or she hadn't told him, but one way or the other Gil knew he wouldn't be able to eat or sleep until he figured it out.

It was getting late, but perhaps if he hurried he may be able to make it back to the market. Maybe it was on the ticket. Surely it was. They wouldn't have just put 217 Willow Street on there would they? Didn't his boss always put the name beside the address?

He wasn't sure; he had never paid attention to the name. Gil knew everyone in town and everyone knew him so there was no need in reading the whole ticket. Normally they just told him to deliver the order to Mrs. Becket or Mr. Waddell or who-ever and he would just naturally know where to go.

This order was different, if there had been a name on the ticket, either he never recognized or paid more attention to the address than the name. "It was a strange name..." he then realized that he was talking out loud. "Why can't I think of that name?" Gil asked aloud again.

He rushed as fast as he could across town to the market. The lot didn't belong to Mr. Mickelson and normally Gil would pull in the spot designated for delivery, but he was in much too big a hurry to worry about getting the right spot. The sign on the front of the door read, "Closed." He was too late, for some reason, the store had closed early. "Why are you closed?" Gil yelled. Mr. Mickelson never closed early, never!

There he sat, right in front of the door, desperately wanting, no needing, to find the most important piece of information in the world and he was too late. He had been so focused on getting to the store in time that he had failed to realize the parking lot was nearly filled to capacity. Even his delivery spot was taken. He looked for a moment, thinking that perhaps he was at the wrong place. Maybe he had gone to the wrong building, no that was foolish, he knew better than that. Again he looked toward the front door of Mickelson's store thinking of how devastating it was to be this close to finding out what Macey's last name was, only to be locked out.

Gil could see the town clock from where he was parked and noticed that it was barely 7:00 pm. "What day is this?" he asked himself. It was Wednesday. "Why would they have closed so early on a Wednesday?" "I wonder if something happened to Mr. Mickelson after I left today?" Again talking to himself. He looked back toward the door of the market hoping that maybe he would see someone moving around inside. "Maybe Leo is still cleaning the place?" He thought aloud. With that he jumped out of the truck and bolted to the door and as he got closer to the door, he finally saw the note; "Closing early today, going to Revival!" "What?" Asked Gil. "Going to revival? What is Revival and was it so important that Mr. Mickelson would close the market for it? "

Gil stood there wondering where this "revival" was and why hadn't he heard about it? He started back to his truck when again he saw just how full the parking lot was, but where was everyone at? He asked out loud, "If the store was closed then why would anyone, much less half the town, be parked here?"

Mickelson's store shared the parking lot with the "five and dime" and an old "Holy Roller" church. That wasn't the name of it, but that is what everyone in town called it. The name of the church was of little importance to Gil; all that mattered right then was why all of these people were at the five and dime. "Are they having a sale?" Gil asked out-loud.

For the moment at least he had forgotten about Macey and was beginning to get a little concerned. "How could something this big be going on under my own nose and me not know about it?" he said. "What did I miss and how?" he asked himself.

Suddenly his thoughts were interrupted by the sound of singing. It was the most beautiful voice he had ever heard! It was as though he was listening to an angel. Gil stood there looking toward the five and dime trying to figure out where the crowd was and more importantly who was singing. It was evident that it wasn't coming from the old store, its lights were out and even when they were on, there wouldn't be any singing coming from it. For the next few minutes Gil found himself transfixed on that voice. It sounded so familiar though he couldn't imagine why. Now, like a moth being drawn to a flame, Gil began walking toward the sound of what he was sure was an angel from God.

CHAPTER 4

SOMETHING GOT AHOLD' OF GIL

The windows were open on the "Holy Roller" church. Inside he could see people fanning themselves with Carson's Funeral Home fans. They were the same fans that his mom had used when they sat in the funeral home for grandpa Oliver's memorial. Gil could remember how stifling hot it was that day. The parlor was packed for the funeral and the heat mixed with all of the perfumes and colognes was enough to take your breath away. He wasn't sure if everyone had been fanning to cool down or to get rid of the smells.

Again he found himself consumed with the melodic voice and the beautiful sound of the piano. Without giving it a second thought, he made his way up the steps and inside the open door. When he stepped inside the church he realized why this voice sounded so familiar, it was indeed the voice of an angel, it was Macey. She was singing the most beautiful song he had ever heard. He just stood there, staring.

Everything in him had stopped, his mind, his heart, and his lungs. Gilbert Matthew Thompson was smitten and he knew it. Who was she and what was it about her that had impacted him so? Gil tried to find a seat back in the back of the building, but there were none. The only seat that he could find was over on the side about half way up. He slid along the wall. He was watching Macey and trying to walk at the same time and it wasn't easy. When he got to the empty seat he realized that it was right beside Mr. Mickelson. Gil nodded and then sat down, still transfixed on Macey.

Just then he remembered the dog was still out in the truck. "Oh well," he thought to himself, "I won't be long." He remembered his mom asking him not to be out late. It was strange to hear her to say that. Gil was never out late and there was no reason to think that today would be any different. They rolled the sidewalks up at sunset in Purdin, he thought. Gil hadn't taken time to clean up and now here he was sitting with all of these people who were dressed in their Sunday best, while he sat there in "play clothes," as his mom liked to call them. Despite feelings of self-consciousness, because of the way he was dressed and the fact that he hadn't combed his hair, Gil knew there was no way he was going to leave.

The singing had ended and he thought he saw Macey glance his way as she made her way to the other side of the church to sit by a woman that he assumed was her mother. As she sat down, the gentleman he had seen just a few hours earlier rose to the pulpit and began to speak. Was it possible that he was the preacher at the "Holy Roller" church and that Macey was his daughter? He was a small man as far as stature goes, probably no more than 5'7" tall and almost frail, at least compared to Gil.

Gil had never been in a Holy Roller church before;

actually, he had only been in church one other time in his life as far as he could remember. It wasn't that his family didn't believe in God. Church was just not something that was a part of their lives, with the exception of Aunt Irene. Grandpa Ollie was as good a man as you could ever meet. Everyone liked him and he liked everyone. He treated everyone with respect, paid his Bills on time and was a hard worker.

Gil had always assumed that church was for all of those people whose lives are messed up. It was okay if you needed it, but he didn't really have a need for it. None of that mattered now; he was half way up to the front of the church, sitting by his boss.

He thought for a moment, "If the guy preaching was Macey's dad and I was to get up and leave, what would that do for my chances with Macey?" What was he thinking? He didn't know anything about her, let alone think that he had a chance with her. All at once his mind was snapped back to the moment and it felt as though his heart was beating through his chest. He could hear it pounding in his ears.

The preacher was a small man, probably no more than 5'6' or so. He had thick black hair and it was greased back on his head. His eyes were ablaze and his voice thundered. Gil wondered where such a small man got such a big voice. The preacher was preaching with such authority that Gil felt his legs beginning to tremble. He hadn't been listening and had no idea how long the man had been talking, but now it was like every distracting thought had vanished.

It was as though everyone had left the building and he was sitting there by himself. It seemed like it was just he and the preacher. The gentleman was talking straight to him, he was telling him things that both scared him and filled him with hope. Gil looked around, certain that, if there was anyone left in the church they were all looking at him. To his amazement they were as tuned in to the sermon as he was. Some were saying "Amen!" Others would occasionally shout out, "Praise God!" He even saw Mr. Mickelson lift his hand and waive a white handkerchief at the preacher. None of that mattered. They could have been doing somersaults in the isle and swinging from the rafters, it wouldn't have made a difference.

Suddenly the excitement of the service reached a crescendo as people began to stand and lift their hands. Some were just sobbing uncontrollably. What in the world was going on? Gils hands were sweaty, his legs were still physically shaking and his heart felt like it was being squeezed. He watched as several people he had gone to school with, got up and went to the front of the church and just fell down on their knees. The preacher was telling everyone how much God loved them and that if they would ask Him, He would save them. He had no idea what that even meant, but it was an offer he couldn't refuse. Gil jumped up out of his seat and before he knew what hit him, he was not just kneeling, but was on his face on the floor. He was calling on a God he had never known and asking Him to be his savior.

Tears were pouring from his eyes and he didn't care if anyone saw him or heard him. Gilbert Matthew Thompson was crying out to God and he knew that God was not only listening, but that He was answering his prayers. Gone was the pain of those days when he would stand out by the road and wait for his dad, knowing that he wasn't coming. Gone was the pain of never knowing what his life could have been like if he had a normal family. Gone also, were all of the feelings of guilt and a weight that he didn't even know he had carried. He felt as light as a feather and freer than he could have imagined! He was lifting both hands toward heaven and shouting to the top of his voice what he heard Mr. Mickelson say earlier, but with more enthusiasm and volume, "Praise God! Praise God!" Over and over he shouted it. Tears of joy ran down his face as he rejoiced over this wonderful change he was experiencing.

After some time had passed and the crowd began to disperse Gilbert stood there with a handkerchief in his hand wiping away tears. He wasn't even sure where it had come from, "hopefully it was Mr. Mickelson's," he thought. Finally Gil turned toward the back door and to his surprise the preacher met him. He had been there the whole time praying with Gil. He knew someone was praying for him, but until then didn't know who it was. The preacher wrapped his arms around Gil and gave him the biggest hug he had ever got. Again the tears started flowing as they hugged and praised God together for what the Lord had done that night. The church was empty for the most part; it was just Gilbert, the preacher and a couple of elderly ladies. The women had their hair put up in some big piles on their head and any other day Gil would have gotten a laugh out of how strange it looked, but today, today they looked like...well, they looked like God. The preacher invited him back the next night and he assured him that he would be there. As a matter of fact, a herd of horses could not have kept him from the place. Not because he knew that Macey would be there, but because he knew that God would be there.

When Gil got to the truck, ole Rex was snuggled up in the seat right where he had left him and was sound asleep. The windows were down and the key was still on, and the truck was still in neutral, but the truck was dead. In the confusion, excitement or whatever it was that gripped him that night, he had forgotten to shut off the truck. He guessed it had just sat there idling until it ran out of gas. Strangely enough it didn't matter, not tonight. Gil pushed his grandpa's old Chevy to the nearest parking spot and he and Rex headed off toward home on foot.

CHAPTER 5

HAZEL AND IRENE

"Where is Gilbert?" "It's not like him to be out this late." Hazel screamed. She was the only one there, but that didn't keep her from talking out loud. She had paced the floor, looked out the door and the window a thousand times. Finally she sat down in her daddy's chair and even though she tried not to, she found herself fearing the worst. What if he had been in an accident? Hazel wondered. She refused to let her mind go there. Rex was gone too, so that means Gil and Rex were probably out squirrel hunting, she surmised. The she saw her dad's shotgun leaning against the wall in the corner, so there was no way they were hunting. Perhaps Gil had taken the dog out to run in the woods. That wouldn't be a stretch since it was one of Gilberts favorite past times. Even if that were the case, they surely wouldn't be out this late. As she sat there wondering about all of the possible scenarios that may explain why he hadn't come home, she couldn't help, but think of how her daddy must have felt that night so many years earlier.

Hazel's life had been filled with more questions than answers. Her mother had passed away shortly after she was born and although her dad had talked to her about how wonderful her mother had been and how much she loved her girls, there was a hole in her heart that she thought would never be filled. Her dad was always her hero. When someone mentioned Oliver Trommel she had always felt a sense of pride. He was a rock. Even though he had lost his beloved wife after only four years of marriage, his quiet demeanor and contentment as well as a deep dedication to her had kept him from ever remarrying.

Hazel and her sister Irene, who was only a year and two months older than her, along with their daddy, had made the best of what was at times a difficult, but rewarding life. Irene, because she was the oldest, had always tried to mother Hazel and at times that was tremendously annoying. She knew that her sister meant well, but one can only take so much of that. Irene had gotten married when she was only 15. She had married into a very wealthy family and quickly became disconnected from Hazel. That was okay, because the last thing she wanted as a teenager was to have to put up with her sister who was barely older than her, trying to act like she was her mom. Irene had done that her entire life.

They were never close, the way that sister's should be. When Irene and her husband Robert moved away from Purdin it was really no big deal, at least not to her. To Oliver though, it was like losing another part of her mom and he seemed to go through the grieving process all over again. Hazel had wished that she could console him, but only time could heal those wounds. She later understood that the grief that she had seen in her daddy was really the hurt that he had never let go of following her mother's death. It was less about Irene moving; after all they were only moving 30 miles away. Thirty miles at the time seemed, at least to her, as if she had moved to a different country.

She could remember hearing Irene come home that Thursday afternoon with the news of Roberts's promotion and subsequent move. "Daddy," Irene had said, "Robert and I are going to be moving. He has taken a job over in Salyersville and although we would love to stay here, it is just not possible." Oliver had insisted that they rethink their decision but he knew that it was a great opportunity and he certainly couldn't blame his son-in-law for wanting to go. Irene had told him, "Daddy, we will be back at least once a month so it's not like you are never going to see me again." That seemed to help and, true to her word, her and Robert came back to Purdin once a month.

Normally they would come in on a Friday evening; they would either stay with Robert's family or at her house. She should have looked forward to their visits, but that was not the case, she actually dreaded them. Oddly enough, Hazel found herself wishing that Irene were there right now. The sun had set hours earlier and Hazel tried with all of her might to remember where it was that Gilbert usually went to run the dog. "What if he has fallen and is laying out there in the woods and is not able to get home?" She thought. Again she broke into to tears at the thought that something may have happened to her Gil.

At once she heard footsteps on the front porch and turned to see the door open. It was Gilbert and the look on his face was as though he had seen an angel. "Momma," he said, "It's okay, don't cry. I'm fine." "Where have you been son?" She asked. Together they sat down and Gil told her the whole story. He told her about 217 Willow and about the beautiful girl that sings like an angel and how that in an effort to find out what her last name was, he found Jesus. Then it dawned on him, "Oh mom, can you believe it, I still never found out what her last name is!" Gil said aloud.

Hazel sat there for a moment in silence as she watched her son's face glowing. She could visibly see the change that had taken place in him that day. She wondered if it were Jesus or Macey that had caused it, but in her heart she knew that it was probably a combination of the two.

CHAPTER 6

IRENE AND ROBERT

Irene and Robert had been married for nearly five years. She had a round face with green eyes and her mom's curly dishwater blonde hair. She wished that she looked like Hazel. Hazel had her daddy's dark skin color and flowing brunette hair. Irene was always jealous, at least until she started having to braid it. It took forever and Hazel always wanted her hair in a braid. One thing she never missed was, having to take care of her sister.

Getting married at 15 years of age seemed like such a good idea at least to a 15 year old, but the reality of the matter was much more difficult. Roberts's family was well to do, but that certainly never played in to her desire to marry him.

Her and Robert met when she was just a freshman and as she would always say, "It was love at first sight." They knew that they were going to be together forever. He graduated high school the year they got married. Throughout school, a lot of the kids had made fun of Robert's red hair and freckles. Then when he was a senior, he had a growth spurt, which caused them to be a little nicer to him. He was tall and lanky when they were first married and had the looks of a businessman. He made sure that his shirts were always pressed and his trousers were always crisp. Irene called him her "red-hair debonair." He was suave and well groomed and much more mature than all of the other boys who had liked her. When they would go walking he never tried to hold her hand, he was just content to walk along side her and listen to her tell about her dreams. Irene had lost her mother when she was only three years old and had to learn very early how to help out around the house.

The most difficult thing for Irene to learn, was, how to be a mom. When you are only a child yourself that is no small task. She was changing her baby sisters' diapers when she was barely out of her own. It was hard, but her daddy had carried most of the weight and always tried to keep her from feeling the pressure her mother's death had caused. She remembered momma, but those memories had faded over the years. Anna Marie Trommel was the most beautiful woman in the world as Irene recalled. She was a petite lady with blond hair and blue eyes and the most captivating smile. Perhaps some of the things that she recalled were mostly from stories her daddy had told her, but either way they were locked into her mind as though she remembered them herself.

The truth was there was little that she did remember. There was one memory however and it was crystal clear, it was a memory that Irene had tried to forget a million times. She remembered what it felt like when her momma first got sick and how quickly she went down hill. It seemed that one day she was picking flowers with her and the next day she watched as they gathered around the bedside and momma was gone. Her and her daddy and a little one-year-old baby were left all alone. She even remembered the wake and was amazed by all of the people who had come to the house.

There were so many people Irene didn't know. It seemed as though each of them felt the need to pick her up and squeeze her. At first she enjoyed the attention, but she remembered how annoying it became after 20 strangers insisted on patting her on the head. Those memories had begun to fade and for the most part she felt okay with that.

Irene never really knew what to do with herself. She never really had the opportunity to be a little girl and I guess you could say that she even resented her little sister for requiring so much attention. Irene tried not to be ugly toward Hazel but it seemed like all that she ever got to do was pack a baby around on her hip or feed her or listen to her cry when she didn't get what she wanted. Maybe that was the reason that they had never been close. Perhaps it was all her fault and that resentment actually may have made marriage seem all the more attractive to her.

When she and Robert announced their engagement, it was as though a ton of weight was lifted off of her shoulders. She was finally going to be free from the pressures of taking care of everyone else. No more cooking and cleaning and doing laundry on that old washer. Irene was going to be Mrs. Irene Turner and she was finally going to be able to walk out of that house and she didn't care if she ever went back. Of course she did care, but for the moment she dreamed of her and her knight in shining armor riding off into the sunset and living happily ever after. She never dreamed that life wasn't really like the books had described and that she was in for some very difficult days ahead.

When they were first married, Irene and Robert lived with his parents and his four brothers, who were obnoxious, to say the least. Those boys were into everything and it seemed that they were trying to make her lose her mind. They did anything they could do to irritate or aggravate her. When she would complain to Robert, he would seem oblivious to it and would just brush it off. "Kid's will be kids," he would say. There was no privacy and at times she longed to be back home. "Maybe her little sister's whining and crying wasn't so bad after all," she thought. The Turner's house only had three bedrooms, which was quite large by many standards, but much too small for her and Robert to ever have any time alone.

When Irene would feel like she had reached the end of her rope, she would climb out of the upstairs window onto the roof and lay as flat as she could so no one would see her and talk to her momma. She longed for some words of inspiration or encouragement from someone, but never seemed to find any, certainly not from Roberts' mom. Elizabeth was a different sort; she was very snooty and always made Irene feel inferior. She remarked one time how that having her in the house was like having another child to raise. Irene was no child, she had spent her whole life being a mother and deeply resented that Mrs. Turner didn't recognize her maturity.

There on the rooftop Irene made plans that were larger than the night sky. She dreamed of her and Robert having their own house and how it would be when he would come in from work. She would have dinner ready and they would spend the evening sitting out on the porch, sipping tea and enjoying each other. Probably a little too idealistic, but at least she wouldn't have to take care of her little sister or put up with Robert's mother and brothers. Irene often wondered what life would have been like if she had a mother. She thought about her friends, whose mom's brushed their hair and bought them frilly dresses or had tea parties with them. How different that was from her life. It's not that she had it rough, quite the contrary, her dad had provided very well and they never lacked for anything, except a mother. That was not his fault and it wasn't hers either. At times she would find herself getting bitter at God for taking her mom, but the thought of that was strange considering the fact that she didn't really believe there was a God. If there was, he had never been a part of her life. They never went to church or discussed religious things at all and that was fine with her. It was just one less thing to have to worry about. "Besides," Irene mused, "what kind of god would take a little girls mother away from her?"

As she lay there on the roof and stared at the night sky she couldn't help but think of how lonely her daddy must have been after the death of her mother. He never really talked much about being lonely, but then again, how do you talk to your little girls about how badly you miss their mother. She would see him staring at her pictures or walking around the house aimlessly. There were times that he would just look out the window and brush tears away. Irene knew how that felt too. Sometimes she would go in and lie on her momma's pillow and try to smell the perfume that she always wore. Sometimes she would try to pretend that her momma was talking to her, and she would answer. Hazel would ask her who she was talking to and Irene would just tell her to mind her own business.

Then Irene thought of how she had pushed her

little sister away and at times had been downright mean to her. Hazel was a good sister, but again Irene reminded herself how unfair it was that she should have to be a mom and didn't get to be a little girl. Life had not been fair to Irene. God, whoever he was, had not been fair to Irene. That night Irene decided to just dismiss the notion of God altogether. He had offered her no solace, no comfort and no help thus far, so why expect his help now. Feeling as frustrated as she had been when she first climbed out onto the roof, Irene slid across the shingles and to the open window.

When she got back in the house, she was just getting ready to slip down the stairs for a glass of milk when Robert came in. He had the biggest grin she had seen in a long time and he grabbed her and wrapped his arms around her and swung her in a circle and said, "Irene, I have great news!" Irene, although a little dizzy and having been totally caught off guard by her excited husband asked, "Robert Turner, what in the world has gotten into you and what kind of news do you have?" "Irene," he said, "I was offered a job over in Salyersville!" "It is a great offer and what's more, there is a house that the company owns and it is a part of the deal," By now Robert was almost shouting. By his tone she realized that he was as excited to get a place of his own as much as she had been. He continued, "Irene Turner, we are going to have a place of our own!" He told her about the job and what it would entail and how much it would pay, but none of that mattered to

37

her.

All that she could think of was a place that she could call home away from Purdin and away from her mother-in-law and those boys! Irene was ready to move that night, but Robert told her that it was going to be a couple of weeks before the house would be ready. He told her that he would have to travel back and forth for the first week or find a place to stay there until the house was available. Irene responded, "Oh no you don't Robert! You aren't leaving me in this house by myself while you stay there. If you are getting out of here than so am I." "Irene, calm down now, you could even stay at your dad's house if you don't want to stay here." "No!" She demanded. "I am not going back to daddy's house either. I am going with you if I have to sleep in the car or under the stars I will, but if you are moving, then I am moving." Robert tried to settle his young wife down, but he could see this was not a battle he could win, so he just wrapped his arms around her and assured her, "We will find a way to make this work, and don't worry, I won't leave you here." Irene was so excited she could hardly sleep that night.

She got up early the next morning and told Robert that she wanted to drive to Salyersville to see if there were any apartments available there. He said, "Let me ask my boss if I can get off work early and we can drive over together." That was even better, she thought. The day seemed to drag along forever and Irene, tired of pacing the floor, decided to walk to Robert's work and wait for him by the car. She arrived at about the same time that he was heading out the door. He never said anything, but his laughter told it all. He knew she wanted out of that house and he knew she couldn't wait to start a life of their own, so why was he surprised that she had walked across town to meet him? The trip to Salyersville was the fastest trip they had ever taken. They were so excited and talked incessantly about how wonderful it would be to finally be on their own. They were going to be away from his family and her family.

For the first time since they were married, they were going to be able to be husband and wife. They were going to live happily ever after, just like in the fairy tales.

CHAPTER 7

MATTHEW THOMPSON

The first time Hazel had seen Matthew Thompson; she was walking down the lane by her house. She had been up the lane delivering some eggs to Mrs. Mueller. It was a spring day and the trees were beginning to bud, there were flowers popping up all along the lane. She had been preoccupied with a neighbor's dog that was barking incessantly at her from the other side of a fence. She hadn't paid a speck of attention to the stranger in the black car that had slowed down and seemed to be following her.

As he pulled up along side of her, he hung his head out of the window and smiled at her. "Hey honey," he said, "Would you like a ride, it looks like that dog is about to climb that fence after you?" He knew that wasn't going to happen, but it didn't stop him from trying to use it to help the cause. Hazel returned a smile but politely declined the invitation for the ride. She knew that dog wasn't going to climb the fence and that if she did she wouldn't bite her. Miss Mollie's dog would be more apt to lick someone to death, rather than bite, but she must admit, the ole girl sure sounded mean. She continued walking and the guy stayed right with her, smiling at her and talking. "What's your name? He asked. "My name is Hazel," she said. "That is a beautiful name, miss Hazel," he continued, "why, that happens to be the color of my eyes." There was just something about his tone that made her feel at ease. Hazel wished that she lived much further down the lane so that the conversation could continue, but she had reached the edge of the path that led to her house.

He was a charmer, to say the least, and even though she didn't know anything about him other than that he had black hair, "hazel eyes" and a black car, she was love-struck. As she turned to walk down the path and away from the lane, she smiled at him and said, "This is my house and I have to get home, my daddy is expecting me."

The black car rolled to a stop and he opened the door and stepped out onto the gravel lane. He seemed to be 10 foot tall as he stood there, smiling and reaching out his hand toward her. He said, "My name is Matthew Thompson and I would like to ask you for a date." Clearly taken aback by his boldness and somewhat surprised at her response, Hazel said, "Well Matthew Thompson, I just might think about that." Then she turned once again toward the house and walked away.

She wanted to look back and see what his response was, but she dare not seem too anxious or excited. She listened to hear the car door shut. She remembered thinking that maybe he would follow her toward the house, but heard neither. She supposed he had just stood there and watched her as she rounded the corner and went into the back door of the house. "That was strange," she thought aloud to herself. "Strange but interesting," she grinned. "I just might think about it, what kind of response was that?" She said. Well, Hazel would certainly think about it, as a matter of fact, that is all that she would be able to think about.

Hazel tried not to act differently, but it was clear that something had been awakened in her. She had never met the guy; she figured it was probably because he was quite a bit older than her. It didn't matter anyway, he was probably not serious about going on a date, so she decided the best thing to do was to forget about it. There were times though that she would find herself standing out by the lane or looking for a reason to be outside, in the event that this tall dark stranger would come back by.

Several weeks had passed and Hazel had said nothing to anyone about Matthew Thompson. Even though she couldn't get him off of her mind, she just went about her daily routines as though the conversation had never happened. There was no way her daddy would allow her to date someone that he never knew, and she was certain her daddy didn't know him. She was wrong about that, but right about her assumption that her daddy wouldn't approve of the relationship. She would later find out that everyone, but her knew Matthew Thompson.

He had a pretty bad name there in Catawba County, actually he was known by every lawman in the western half of the state. He always seemed to stay one step ahead of them. When it looked as thought they had him and would finally bring him to justice, he would somehow slip through their net. Everyone knew that he was running moonshine and yet every time that he was pulled over, his car was empty. They didn't know that he had an extra large gas tank and that only a third of it contained fuel, the other two-thirds would carry about 18 gallon of shine.

From the time that he had been old enough to drive and had something to drive, Matthew drove fast and hard. There seemed to be a mystique about him, that heir of mystery caused him to be popular with the young ladies and hated by their fathers. He had been duly warned by more than one daddy to stay away from their daughters, but Matthew was going to have to learn the hard way.

He had been given a delivery that required him to go through Purdin. He had made that run plenty of times, but this would be a trip that he would not soon forget. Matthew seemed to leave a trail of broken hearts everywhere he went, and Purdin was no exception. He was a player, and although he considered himself pretty lucky, his luck was about to run out. He knew that he had to be extremely cautious because of the load he was carrying, and as a result he had chosen to take the back roads that day.

When he turned off of route 17 onto Maple lane he couldn't help but notice the young lady who was walking along the side of this picturesque gravel road that was lined with Maple trees. Matthew knew that he didn't have time to stop, but after glancing in his rear-view mirror and realizing that no one was following him, he pulled along side her and tried to strike up a conversation. In his usual debonair way, he asked her for a date, but unlike all of the other girls, she told him that she would only think about it and then quickly went into the house.

Thinking that he was losing his touch and that he had wasted enough time, Matthew got back in the car and gave it the gas. As he did he noticed the sheriffs cruiser coming in behind him on the lane. He tried to keep his cool, but he knew that he was heavy on the juice, and a little light on fuel. If he got into a race with the deputy he would likely run out of gas before he could shake him.

The deputy was gaining on him and it seemed obvious that there was nothing he could do, but play it cool and hope for the best. Matthew let up on the gas and the deputy quickly passed him and continued down the lane. He breathed a sigh of relief as he thought about what he would have done had he been pulled over. Generally Matthew was laid back and not easily shaken, but today was different. Not only was his tank full of shine, but there was some in the trunk as well. This was going to be a short run or he never would have agreed to do it, besides, he mused, 'it was good money'.

As he rounded the curve leading just before highway 3, Matthew noticed a newer looking truck had pulled in behind him. It seemed to jump up on him pretty quickly. He sped up just enough to let who ever this was, know that he was paying attention. Once again the truck driver was nearly in his trunk.

Matthew had become so focused on the truck that he nearly ran through the middle of two squad cars that were blocking the lane. When he locked up the car, he slid sideways coming to rest within a foot of the police car that had passed him moments earlier. As he did the truck pulled within an inch of his passenger door.

There was no where to go, standing there in front of him with guns drawn were three of the biggest men he had ever seen. Two of them were clearly lawmen, but the other was an older guy, maybe mid to late forties. Before he knew what was happening, the older guy reached in the window and pulled Matthew out of the car by the hair. He screamed profanities at him and threw him around like a rag doll. Matthew never stood a chance and the lawmen weren't trying to stop the guy, who was clearly going to kill him.

They just watched this man pummel him. Finally the man slammed Matthew up against a squad car and held him there by the neck. Matthew honestly thought that he was going to kill him. For a moment he actually wished that this had something to do with the shine he was hauling, but he knew it didn't.

When he was ready to pass out from the choking that he was receiving, the man let him go and he fell to the ground. As Matthew crumpled to the ground, he was gasping and coughing. This didn't seem to satisfy his assailant. The man screamed a thousand more profanities at him as he continued punching him. Matthew muttered, "Who are you and why are you trying to kill me?" "Punk, if I wanted to kill you, you would already be dead!" The man replied. "Her name is Helen, she is my daughter and if you ever touch her again I will finish what I have started. You got that?" With that the man kicked him hard in the stomach and Matthew blacked out.

When he awoke, he fully expected to be in jail, or dead. To his surprise, he was still laying there in the ditch where the man had left him. Every inch of his body hurt. Normally it was he who was giving the beatings. He had never been on the receiving end, but today he was the recipient of the worst beating of his life. Matthew finally pulled himself to the car and to his surprise the keys were still in it. He managed to drag himself in behind the wheel, when he looked in the mirror he saw just how badly he was beaten.

Blood had dried from both nostrils; his lips were swollen so badly that he couldn't even talk. His hazel eyes stung with blood and his proud look was anything but proud now. He started the car and pulled away, south onto highway 3.

Matthew told himself that he would never use that lane again and the quicker he could unload his stuff the better. If he never saw Purdin again it would be too soon. After unloading his car and emptying the reservoir, Matthew sped back to Inez and pulled into the shed behind his dad's house. He didn't think his dad would be home, but if he were it wouldn't matter because in all likelihood he would probably be passed out. Sure enough his dad lay there on the couch overtaken by the 'shine' Matthew had supplied him with. He was out cold as a cucumber and that was fine with Matthew. He didn't want to chat or answer a bunch of questions. All that Matthew wanted was a bath and to get some rest.

The pain was excruciating. When he walked into the bathroom and began to pull his shirt off, he realized why he was so sore. His ribs and stomach were nearly black. He washed as well as he possibly could and then went to bed. For the next couple of weeks Matthew laid low, not because he wanted to, but because he was too sore to move. The thought of Purdin made him wince with pain. Thankfully a lot of the beating had seemed to fade from his memory, one thing that hadn't, was the sound of the man's voice that had nearly killed him.

He lay there hearing those words replay over and over in his mind, "Her name is Helen!" Said the man. "Helen?" He could barely even remember Helen. "She was a one-timer," that much he could recall. He couldn't remember what she even looked like, but one thing was certain, he said, "I have no intentions of going any where near her or Purdin if I have anything to say about it."

His thoughts were interrupted by the sound of cursing, and the door to his room burst open. "Get out of bed boy, you gotta make a run." His boss yelled. "We aren't paying you to sleep, now get up and meet me at the barn in 25 minutes or you will wish you had!" Although still in tremendous pain, Matthew knew better than back talk or argue. He hurried as much as possible to get dressed and rushed to the barn. When Matthew arrived at the barn, they filled his car with shine. Then they told him he had a run to make and it had to be quick. "I need you to get this to Purdin..." Matthew cringed when he heard where he was told to go. Of all of the places on earth, this was the last place he wanted to be seen. He wasn't nearly as afraid of law enforcement as he was of running in to Helen's dad again.

He stopped in at Mel's service station and had the attendant top off his car. He knew that it would only hold 6 gallons, but he acted surprised every time. "Only 6 gallons huh, must be something wrong with my gas gauge?" Matthew remarked. The Attendant took his $1.30 cents and reached in his pocket to give him his change. "You know sir" the attendant remarked, "come to think of it, that is the most I ever put in your car. Why don't you pull in and let Mel check to see if something might be wrong with your tank." Matthew hurriedly got in the car and told the attendant to keep the change and muttered something unintelligible to him and then drove away. He knew there was something wrong with his tank, but he sure wasn't going to allow Mel or anyone else to probe around in it.

He had heard that Mel was some kind of snitch or

something, and he would get gas there just to try to stay on his good side. Six gallon of Ethel was just enough to get him to Purdin and back if he kept his foot out of the gas. That would prove hard to do for two reasons, one, because he liked fast driving and two, he was always looking for a way to show off in front of a lady. He dreaded going any where near that town. The thought of running in to a mad dad was somewhat over-taken by the thought of Hazel. True, he hadn't given her another thought, but since he was going to be in town, maybe he would run into her.

After making his drop, Matthew decided to hang out in town for a few minutes, in the event that Hazel happened to be there. He assured himself that, barring a chance meeting with her; he wasn't about to get out of the car. Much to his surprise, there in front of the general market sat Hazel in an old pickup. Matthew wondered for a moment what she was waiting on and then decided to make his move.

He opened the door and hurried across the street to the passenger door of her truck. Clearly he had startled her. In an attempt to ease her concerns, he offered to buy her a pop. He wasn't one to take no for an answer, and in a few minutes he had convinced her to meet him for a date the next time he was in town. "Two weeks," he said. He really didn't know where he would be in two weeks, but if it worked out, that would be fine and if not? "Oh well," he thought.

Matthew didn't like to be in this part of the county, but he was making easy money and he might as well make the most of it. As he was leaving town he stopped to top off his tank and quickly got back to Inez, parked the car and headed in to get his pay. Normally getting paid was no big deal, there would be an envelope waiting for him, tucked under an old water bucket just inside the door. He would get his money and head out for a night on the town, but tonight wasn't going to be a normal night.

CHAPTER 8

A NEW HOME IN SALYERSVILLE?

"Welcome to Salyersville, population 846" Robert said. Salyersville was not much of a town, it was only about half the size of Purdin but Robert and Irene were so excited to see their new town. The first thing on the agenda was to drive to the address of the house that would soon be theirs. When Irene saw it, she began to cry. "Is this it Robert?" She asked. "Yes, I think so Irene." He answered. It was perfect as far as they could tell, green shingle siding, a wrap around porch with a porch swing on the corner. There were flowers all along the front of the house and it even had a picket fence on one side of it. "Robert," said Irene, "this is more than I could have ever imagined. Do we have to wait two weeks to move in?" "Yes," he said, "the people who live there have to move out before we can move in, unless..." He paused. "Unless what?" Hazel asked. "Unless, you want to move in with them." He said with a grin. "No thank you! I am not living with anyone else, ever!" Irene declared.

As they drove through town the noticed a sign out in front of a storefront building on main street that said, "Apartment for rent." Robert brought the car to a stop and they both jumped out, eager to find out if the apartment was still available. It was an upstairs apartment and was situated directly above a furniture store. They were thrilled to find out that it was still available.

The owners at weren't too excited about renting it for such a short time frame, but they could see how desperate Irene and Robert were, so they acquiesced. "We will have to charge you for a full month, even if you are only here for a week or two." Said Mr. Lands. "That will be fine" Irene replied. "Now let me explain some things before you we sign the paperwork." He said. "Lands furniture store has been in business for a long time and we are very proud of the good name that we have in this town. We will not allow any drinking or smoking in our apartment. The smell of cigarettes get's in the furniture and it won't come out!" He Continued. "We close early on Wednesday evening, and you will have to use the back entrance, I'll show you where it is in a moment. On Wednesday's and Sundays we use this entry way for church services." Mr. Lands explained. "Church services?" Irene blurted out. "Yes ma'am." he replied. "Is that a problem?"

Before Irene could say another word Robert quickly assured him that it wasn't a problem, but that his wife just wanted to make sure she heard him plainly. "She is sometimes a little hard of hearing." Robert added, as he tried to cover the clear shock that his wife had expressed. "Well, that will come in handy on Sunday's and Wednesday evenings I guess." said Mrs. Lands. "We have a pretty good group of folks that gather down here and they sure do love their Lord. You all would be welcome to join us for worship services some time." She said. "Oh well...uh um, I guess we will have to see about that." Said Robert; although he knew there was no chance that was going to happen. Mr. and Mrs. Lands were showing them around the apartment and explaining where they could put their furniture and such like, but all Irene was thinking was, "You are wasting your time with all of this, we aren't moving anything but the bare necessities in, because in two weeks we are moving in to the house over on Mulberry St." Her and Robert just smiled and try to act interested. They walked through the apartment and then down the back stairway that led to the side entrance. "This is where you will come and go on Sunday's and Wednesday's." Exclaimed Mrs. Lands

"This is where you will park on the weekends," explained Mr. Lands. "It gets a little crowded out front." That was an understatement, as they would soon find out. When all of the tour was over, Robert and Irene followed Mr. and Mrs. Lands through the furniture store and then through the "church" to a back office. They signed the agreement for their new apartment and paid the down payment.

As they were preparing to leave, Mrs. Lands stopped them and said, "Do you mind if we pray with you kids before you head back to Purdin?" Without waiting for an answer, she and Mr. Lands grabbed them by the hands and began to pray. "Our heavenly Father, we thank you for the chance to rent this apartment to Robert and Irene. We bless your name for bringing them into our lives and allowing us to show them your love. I want to thank you Jesus for giving your life on Calvary for us, and showing your great love to us. Now I ask that you would bless them as they make their way back to Purdin. Keep them safe and don't allow any harm to come to them as they travel. Jesus, be with these kid's and show them how much you love them I pray. Amen." She finally finished. Irene tried not to laugh. "I didn't know we were going to get a whole sermon." She thought,

When the prayer ended, they thanked the Lands' for the opportunity to rent the apartment and assured them that they would abide by all of the rules. "We certainly appreciate you and thank you for allowing us to rent on such a short notice and for allowing us to move in quickly. We should be here this Friday and will be moving just the necessities in. Our house should be ready as early as two weeks from today, so we may only be here a week or so." Robert said.

When they got to the car and were sure that they couldn't be heard, Irene started to say something, but

Robert quickly cut her off, "We will only be here for a few days." He must have read her mind. She laughed at the thought of living above a church. "Robert," she said, "I sure hope that house is ready quickly!" "Yeah, me too!" He agreed.

By the time that they had driven by and looked at the house again, and the building where he was going to be working, it was nearly dark. "Can you believe we are going to have our own place Robert?" Irene asked. "It is amazing isn't it sweetheart?" Answered Robert. "I wonder what the inside of the house looks like?" Asked Irene "I don't know, but it has to be better than our bedroom at my parents." He said, knowing how uncomfortable that had become for both of them. "Yeah, and it will definitely be better than living above a church!" She quipped.

They had only gone about a ten minutes out of town when suddenly Robert pulled the car to the side of the road. "What is wrong, Robert?" she asked. "I don't know. I just felt impressed that I should pull over and stop the car." He said. No sooner had he brought the car to the edge of the road that the drivers' side front tire blew out. It literally exploded. Robert and Irene just sat there looking at each other as the front of the car just sank as the air went out of the tire. "What was that?" Irene asked. "We just had a blow out! If I would have kept driving there is no telling what would have happened. We could have had a bad wreck." Robert said, clearly shaken by what had happened. "That was the weirdest thing I have ever experienced in my life. I was just driving along and it's like I heard a voice telling me to pull over. I thought for a moment how strange it was and almost drove on, but I heard it again and I no more than got the car stopped and the tire blew." Said Robert.

"Wow! That was strange!" Irene responded, "Well I guess it's our lucky day, we got an apartment and we didn't have a wreck. Now if we have a spare tire we will really be lucky," Irene said. Thankfully they had a spare and despite the fact that it was now nearly too dark to see to change the tire, Robert got it done and they continued the drive to Purdin.

The next morning, Irene packed what little she had from their bedroom. Robert had to work a half-day, but as soon as he was off, she and Robert loaded everything into the car and headed across town to her dad's house. Irene rushed through the back door and into the house where she found her sister and her dad eating lunch. "Daddy, guess what?" Irene said. "Robert got a new job and we are moving!"

Irene was clearly excited at the prospect of moving and never thought about how that news would affect her dad. He put his sandwich down and tried to act as happy as Irene, but he didn't do a very good job of it. "Where are you moving?" He asked. "We are moving to Salyersville!" Irene replied. "And when is all of this happening?" Asked Oliver. "We are leaving this Friday daddy!" Said Irene. "We are moving into an apartment for now, but in less than two weeks we get to move in to our own house. It is a beautiful house, it's got a porch swing and flowers and a picket fence on one side of it." She continued on and on with a thousand details, none of which was as thrilling to Oliver as it had been to Irene.

Oliver finally interrupted her, "When did you find this out and why didn't you say anything about it? Do you know that Salyersville is a long way away? I don't get to see you very often now and if you move to Salyersville I will never see you." He said, clearly upset. "Daddy, don't worry, we are going to come home on Fridays. The apartment that we are moving into, it's above a furniture store and they have church there on Wednesdays and Sundays. And, since we can't move into it for a couple of weeks, we have decided to come here next Friday if that is okay with you, that way we don't have to be there for church?" Irene continued. "Roberts job is really good daddy, and I can come home as often as I want. We will actually see each other more now than we have in the past year! This is our chance to finally have a place of our own." Irene kept talking without waiting for an answer or response from anyone.

Even if Hazel could have gotten a word in, she wouldn't have. She frankly didn't care if Irene moved to ten-buck-two. Oliver, on the other hand, looked as if someone had killed his best friend. The thought of losing his daughter was almost too much to take. Again and again she and Robert told of the new job and their temporary apartment and the new house that they would be living in. "We get to live in the house rent free Daddy!" Irene said, for the umpteenth time.

After visiting for an hour or so, Robert looked at Irene and said, "Honey, we need to get going or we will be unpacking all night long. Besides, I would rather not be driving that curvy road too late at night, especially after what happened last night."

With that Irene hugged her daddy and told him she loved him, she looked at Hazel and said, "bye," but that was it. Hazel told her good bye and again Irene assured her daddy that they would be back next Friday to stay the night.

Oliver was thrilled at the notion of getting to see his daughter. He told her that he would love to have them stay there any time they wanted. He didn't expect it to happen, but it sounded nice.

Robert and Irene rushed to the car and pulled out of the drive onto the lane that meandered back toward town. It was after 11:00 pm. when they finally got everything unpacked. They made a pallet in the floor for their first night in the new apartment. They were planning to spend the next day, Saturday, looking around town.

They wanted to find the best place to shop for groceries and to see what all was there. Unfortunately the weather didn't cooperate.

At about three in the morning they were awakened

with the clap of thunder and a flash of lightning that was loud enough to wake the dead. It echoed through the empty apartment and shook the wood floor where they were sleeping. The sky was filled with one flash after another and the apartment shook with each new boom of thunder. They had not paid attention to the fact that the firehouse was caddie-corner of the furniture store, but the wail of the siren let them know just how close it was.

They ran to the window as the fire truck pulled away from the open garage and out across town. For the next couple of hours they lay there talking as one wave of storms after another came through. Around five Irene and Robert finally drifted off to sleep and were sleeping quite sound. Suddenly, they were jolted from their sleep with the bang of the heavy door of the furniture store slammed shut.

They both jumped up as though they had been shot. It was nine o'clock in the morning and it sounded like all of Salyersville was furniture shopping downstairs. In truth it was only a couple looking for a new sofa, but the old building evidently wasn't very well insulated and every little sound carried and settled in their apartment, or at least it seemed that way. Robert and Irene sat back down in the floor, contemplating what their next move would be. Robert motioned for Irene to look out the window and said, "I don't think we will be doing any site seeing today, sweetheart. Look how hard it is raining." The rain was still coming down, and showed no sign of letting up.

The street below them was almost a creek as was every other street in town. The Alakwon creek ran along the edge of town and you could tell that it was to point of overflowing its banks. Irene went into the kitchen and fried the only two eggs that they had brought and toasted some bread. They sat back down in the floor and ate their breakfast. Finally at about 1:00 in the afternoon, the weather broke and the sun began to pop out from behind the clouds.

They got ready quickly and made their way down the stairs. They were getting ready to go out to see the sites of Salyersville when they were stopped by Mrs. Lands'. "Good afternoon you two," She said with a smile. "How was your first night in Salyersville? I tell you what; we got some kind of storm last night didn't we? Keller's service station just about got washed away. It sits right there by the Alakwon and when that creek gets up like it did this morning, well let's put it this way, they will be picking up tires all the way down to Purdin. They had to rescue a family from a house on the other side of town. Their house got struck by lightning and caught fire. We haven't heard yet whose house it was, but one of the children evidently died in the fire. The house was burned badly, but with all of the commotion it's hard to know how much damage was done.

A couple of buildings had their roofs damaged by the wind and one had a tree fall across it, but..." she continued, "Thank God most everyone weathered the storm and now it looks like the sun is going to shine on Salyersville." Robert nodded and Irene spoke up, "Well, Robert we had better get going, we have a lot to get done and half the day is gone." They told Mrs. Lands to have a good day and they headed out to "experience" the big city of Salyersville.

As Robert and Irene walked out of the furniture store, Irene looked at Robert with a half grin and said, "Well Robert at least we got the full run down on the weather, a storm damage report and now we know where we can get a spare tire for the car." "Now Irene, she was just trying to make conversation" Robert replied. "I know, I know, but did she really have to tell us about every sign and tree limb in the county that got damaged by the storm?" Quipped Irene. The street was littered with limbs just as Mrs. Lands had said and maybe a little worse.

As they made their way to their car they noticed a limb laying across the roof of the car and at first thought it was much worse than it was. Although the car had a dent and some scratches, it was otherwise unharmed. They were surprised not only by how much damage there was, but also by how large Salyersville was. Their previous trip they had been so preoccupied with seeing the house and Roberts new place of work that they paid little attention to anything else.

On the east side of town they saw where the service station had been flooded and just like Mrs. Lands had said, there were tires strewn everywhere. People were out trying to gather up the tires and help stack them back where they had been. Robert remarked, how nice it would be to be a part of a town where everyone pulled together in the face of a tragedy. "This is going to be a great place to raise our family Irene." He said. Irene grinned, but Robert could tell that Irene wasn't quite as excited as he was at the thought of having a family. "Robert, maybe we could drive back by the house and see if the family has started moving yet?" Irene asked. "They still have until this Friday honey, I don't want them to think that we are trying to run them out of town." He answered. "Oh don't be silly, they didn't even know we were there and it's not like we are going to go ask them if we can help them pack or something. We could just drive by and take a look. Come on, please Robert?" She said with a whine. "Alright, let's go see the house and maybe the neighbors will help us throw their stuff out of the house so we can move in." Robert said jokingly. "Yeah that will be perfect, then we can run back to the apartment and put all of our things in a pillow case and move in today." Irene responded.

As they drove toward the house it was clear that there was a lot more damage on this side of town. There were several houses that had roof damage and trees were split apart and uprooted everywhere. Navigating around the debris proved to be a task, however, the damage to the trees and the debris scattered around was minor compared to what they would see around the corner. As they turned on to

Mulberry Street, they were unprepared for the scene in front of them. The house that was soon to be theirs was gone. The entire back portion of the house had been burnt to the ground and the front was not much better. The fire had been so intense that it had even burned the fence. Everything about the house that made them so desperately want to move here, was now gone. "Oh no Robert, what are we going to do? That's our house, or it was our house. What are we going to do Robert?" Irene asked with her eyes welling with tears. Robert could say nothing; he just put his arm around Irene and held her as they sat there on the side of the street in a daze. "Are we going to have to go back to your parents house? Asked Irene. "No honey, that isn't an option, I would not be able to drive back and forth to work and there is no way that I would put you back in that situation. I saw how happy you were at the thought of moving. I'm not sure what we are going to do; maybe my boss will have some ideas. For now we can get some furniture for the apartment and try to make a home there. We will have to see if it is available for another few weeks while we try to figure it out."

They sat there for a while longer and then headed back to the apartment, feeling dejected. "Well my dear, welcome to our first Saturday in Salyersville," "I know it's not what we had hoped for, but thankfully we have a place to sleep. We just happen to live above a furniture store, so hopefully we can get some furniture for the apartment." Said Robert. "Robert, I know that I have asked you, but we really need to decide what we are going to do. If we can't find a house do you think that this job is such a good deal? We need to call your boss and tell him what has happened so they can find us a place to live. I don't mean to be ugly, but living above a furniture store is fine, but we are going to be living above a church as well.

Have you ever been to church before Robert?" Irene asked. "Well yes, when I was a kid we went to church quite a lot, but that's not the same as living above one I guess" he replied. "How about you, have you ever been to church?" He asked. "Uh, no I don't suppose I have, other than occasionally when I would visit Loretta's house. If it's anything like the church she attends, we won't even know that they are there, other than the slam of that 300 pound door with that loud bell on it. Oh surely they won't use that entrance, will they?" She asked, "I don't know, but I suppose we are worrying too much about it. Right now we just need to find a bed so that we don't have to sleep on that floor. My back is killing me and it would be nice if we could get a table and chairs and maybe a nice comfortable chair that I can sit in while you serve me dinner after while," Robert said jokingly. "How can you joke about it Robert? I was so looking forward to having a house to call our own and now it looks like we are going to be living in that apartment indefinitely." She complained. "Well Irene, at least my brothers aren't moving in with us!" Robert rebuffed. Irene just groaned as she thought of the idea of those boys. "Besides, think about that family that lost everything in that fire. I'm sure that they would love to have an apartment and a place to lay their heads down tonight." Robert continued. "This certainly is not the best of circumstances, but on the bright side, I have a great job and we have a place to live that is warm and dry. We have each other and if you ask me, that's a pretty good situation, even if it is above a church."

I wonder what kind of church it is. I mean, they are meeting in a furniture store lobby so you have to figure it's not a conventional church and I didn't see any stain glass windows. Did you Irene?"

Irene was still busy thinking about Roberts brothers and how difficult it had been for the past year in those cramped quarters and no privacy and how rude Robert's mom could sometimes be. "Did you Irene!" Robert shouted, breaking her concentration. "What Robert? Why did you yell? Did I what?" She asked. "Did you see any stained glass?" He answered. "Where?" Asked Irene. "I was trying to figure out what kind of church they had downstairs and I noticed that I hadn't seen any stained glass. Come to think of it, I don't remember any statutes. There has to be statutes of the saints don't there, if it is really a church. Maybe they have one of those big pipe organs. That would be beautiful wouldn't it sweetheart?" He said, clearly being sarcastic. "Oh Robert, you are crazy. Of course there is no stained glass and no I didn't see any statutes or an organ and if there is an organ I am moving out." She said with a smile.

They were almost back to the furniture store when Irene remembered that they didn't have any thing to fix for dinner. "Oh Robert," she exclaimed, "I need to find a market, we don't have a thing in the apartment to eat." As she finished her request Robert noticed a small grocery store only a block from the apartment. "How about we park the car and walk back down there?" He suggested. "Why don't I run on up to the apartment and you can pick up what we need?" Irene answered.

Robert pulled in behind the furniture store at the spot where they had been told to park, but there was no space available. He pulled across the alley and Irene got out and headed toward the back door of the store. Robert turned to go back to pick up a few items from the market. As Irene neared the door she heard what sounded like someone wailing inside, as a matter of fact it sounded like a whole lot of people were inside the building. She had never heard such groaning in her life. She quickly yelled to Robert, "Robert, quick come here. There is something dreadfully wrong in there and I am afraid to go in." Robert ran quickly to her side. They stood there together trying to figure out if they should go in or perhaps they should go to the police station. After a few moments of bewilderment, Irene followed Robert onto the porch and they walked slowly toward the door.

Not knowing anyone in town was one thing, but all of

the moaning inside the furniture store made things seem a whole lot more strange. When Robert opened the door it swung loose from his hand and slammed into the wall behind it. When it did, some people looked around to see what the noise was, but for the most part they all just stayed where they were, kneeling or lying across the floor. They were crying and praying so intensely that most of them never even heard that massive door hit the wall. Robert looked at his wife; she looked like she had seen a ghost. He grabbed her by the arm and rushed her to the stairway leading to their apartment.

Once inside she began laughing hysterically and crying at the same time. "Robert, what have we got ourselves into? These people are weird! I'm scared Robert, I mean it. I don't think I can stay here. What kind of church is that?" She asked. Robert was baffled as well. "Irene, I am so sorry, if I had known how strange this place was, I would never have agreed for us to stay here." He replied. They were so shook up that they completely forgot about dinner. They just sat there trying to drown out the noise from below. After a couple of hours they realized that things seemed to calm down and Robert bravely stuck his head into the stairwell to make sure that everything was okay.

He motioned to Irene and they walked gingerly down the stairs with every intention to get out the door without being noticed, but to no avail. Mr. Lands stood at the bottom of the steps with one hand outstretched toward Robert and a handkerchief in the other one. "Well hello kids, I didn't hear you come in. If I would have known you were home, I would have asked you to join us for prayer meeting." He said with a tear cascading down his cheek.

He continued, "We don't normally have Saturday prayer, but one of them babies that was in the fire last night was overcome with smoke and he didn't make it. His twin sister did, bless her heart. She is just the tiniest thing you ever saw, but she has a way's to go. We were praying for her and for her momma and daddy. I can't imagine what it would be like to lose a baby. I hope that you all would keep them in your prayers."

Both Robert and Irene stood there stunned and ashamed. How dare they be so judgmental toward these fine folks? They were doing everything they knew to do to help a family that had suffered a horrible tragedy. Although Irene had clearly never liked the idea of having children she certainly could not imagine the pain that the mother of that child must feel. All they had thought of was the inconvenience they were dealing with. Now the loss of a house was nothing, and if they had to live in an apartment then at least they had that, and they had each other.

"Mr. Lands," Robert said, "Irene and I are so sorry. If there is anything that we can do, please let us know. We were on our way out to get something to make for dinner and we would be glad to pick some

MOMENTS-THE STORY OF GIL AND MACEY

things up for that family." Mr. Lands interrupted, "Please call me Walter. My wife and I would like for you to join us for dinner tonight, if you would be so kind." Robert started to say no, but Irene nudged him in the side and instead he said, "Mr. Lands, I mean Walter, Irene and I would be honored to join you." "We live just down the street at 311 Windsor, we will have dinner ready at 6:00 if that will work?" "Certainly, Mr. Lands, I mean Walter." Replied Irene.

They started out the door to go to the market, but Irene stopped. "Walter," she said, "Is there any chance that Robert and I could look at some furniture real quickly? I promise we will make it quick. We don't have much up there and if you would allow it, we would appreciate it." "Well certainly, you kids take all the time you need and when you find what you want we will help you get it up the stairs." He said. He asked them what they were looking for and gave them some directions for finding the best furniture. "Now listen," he said, "don't you pay any attention to the prices, we are going to take good care of you. You just find what you are looking for and then come and get me and before you know it, we'll have your furniture upstairs and it will feel like home."

They tried to look quickly because they only had a couple of hours before they were supposed to go to dinner. When Irene had settled on a small chair for herself and a larger one for Robert, they moved quickly to the bedroom sets. They picked a pretty

one out and found Mr. Lands and just like he had
said, in no time, they had the furniture upstairs and
were rushing around trying to get ready for dinner.

CHAPTER 9

THE MEETING

Hazel woke up earlier than normal that Saturday morning. She had just started driving and had asked her dad if she could drive the truck to town to pick up some things for the house. She also wanted to drive over to the lake where some friends were going to be hanging out. She was surprised that he had agreed to both requests, considering she hadn't driven much.

Hazel quickly got ready and found her daddy out in the workshop. "Daddy," she said, "I'll be gone for a while so don't worry about me." Oliver knew that his daughter was very mature for her age. He had no reason to doubt her. He smiled at her and told her to drive carefully and to enjoy herself. "I have a lot to do around here sweetheart. You take your time and be home before dark." She kissed him on the cheek and ran to the truck, waved anxiously and told him goodbye.

It was less than two miles to town, but she felt like she was taking a much longer journey. She dreamed as she drove down the lane toward town and away from home. She imagined her meeting with Matthew that had happened a few weeks earlier and wondered why she had not seen or heard of him before then. Hazel dare not bring his name up to anyone, she didn't know why, but he was just mysterious enough that at times, she wasn't even sure that it had happened. As she drove up to the front of the market she couldn't help but notice the car that was parked across the street. It was the same car that she had seen a few weeks earlier. Her heart was pounding and fluttering at the same time. She felt like a schoolgirl, which made perfect sense; after all she was a schoolgirl. Her mind was racing a million miles an hour. What if she saw him? He probably wouldn't even remember her. What if he has someone with him, maybe he has a girlfriend with him? She quickly stopped the truck and just sat there.

She sat there wondering if the black car was his. Lost in her thoughts, Hazel was startled by someone tapping on her passenger side window. She jumped and screamed at the same time. "I didn't mean to scare you little miss." Said Matthew. She was embarrassed and startled but not scared. "Well, uh, hello." Hazel said. Matthew walked around to the driver's side of the truck and smiled at her as he leaned into the open window. "I wondered if I would ever see you again. Well, did you think about it?" asked Matthew. "Excuse me." Replied Hazel. "You told me that you might think about a date." He said. "Well, yeah I did think about it and then when I never heard anything from you or saw you anymore I tried to quit thinking about it." Hazel said nervously. "Well?" asked Matthew. "Well, I don't know. I don't really know anything about you and I am not sure that my daddy would agree with the notion. That doesn't mean that I won't, I just don't know if I can say yes." She answered.

MOMENTS-THE STORY OF GIL AND MACEY

"Well, if we can't go on a date maybe I could at least buy you a pop and we could at least talk? I'm in town for a couple of hours and would love to spend it with you." Matthew replied.

Hazel agreed and they walked together Harper's drug store. The next hour or so went by so fast. She kept telling herself, "This is not a date" but in her heart she knew it was. She tried not to think about how her father would feel, since it wasn't a date, it was surely okay. After a while Matthew looked across the table at Hazel and said, "I have to get going, but I want to see you sometime, I really would like to take you out on a real date. We could go for a ride in the car, go out to eat at a nice restaurant and then just sit out under the stars and talk. I will be back in a couple of weeks and if you want, we could meet here in town and go out?

Before she knew it she had said yes. "Yes? What was she thinking?" Hazel thought. Matthew stood and excused himself; he laid some money on the counter and turned to smile at her again before he left. "I will see you in two weeks?" He asked. She nodded yes and watched as he went out the door and ran toward his car. He must have been going 30 miles per hour by the time he got to the end of the street, she thought.

Hazel had been so engrossed with him that she hadn't realized that Irene's friend Naomi was sitting at the table behind her. Hazel couldn't seem to shake the sick feeling that had come over her. Instead of

73

going on out to the lake to meet up with her friends as she had planned, she decided it would be best to just go home. Her mind was racing as she drove back to the house, it was only a couple of miles, but it seemed to take forever.

She couldn't find her father so she walked down by the pond to see if he was there. She needed to talk to him about Matthew, but didn't know if she could bring herself to do it. As she reached the pond she realized that he wasn't there so she just sat there on the edge of the pond under the massive willow. Hazel let her mind wonder. She wondered what her mother would tell her to do. She was concerned that her dad would be upset with her for agreeing to go out with anyone who was not willing to first ask him.

She wasn't trying to be rebellious, but what would it hurt to go on a date with Matthew? "What would Irene think?" She thought. "Then again why did it matter what Irene thinks?" She had never asked if she should go out with Robert nor did she care about how getting married would effect her or her dad. Irene never talked to Hazel about anything, let alone her love life. She just got married and moved away. Hazel thought, "If I want to go out with Matthew, I will do it. If Irene deserves to be happy then so do I."

Hazel sat there for a little while longer just staring and thinking. "Why does this have to be so hard?" She screamed aloud. Her eyes were beginning to burn as she felt the hot tears well up. Was she upset because she didn't have a mother to talk to, or was it because she was sneaking behind her dad's back and she knew it would break his heart? She felt sick to her stomach and she couldn't seem to stop the tears. Suddenly she was snapped back to reality with the voice of her father yelling, "Hazel! Hazel! Where are you? Hazel!" She could hear the fear in his voice. She wiped her tears and tried to dry her face so that he wouldn't know that she had been crying. "I'm down here daddy!" She answered. "I'm down by the pond." He ran down the path toward the pond and Hazel stood up and tried to pull herself together. Oliver came to the edge of the pond, "I was worried sick sweetheart." He said. "I saw the truck, but I couldn't find you... Are you alright dear?" He continued. "Have you been crying? Did someone hurt you?" He asked. "No, I'm fine daddy. I'm just feeling a little nauseated for some reason. I decided it would be best if I came back home instead of going to the lake with the gang." Hazel replied.

Oliver put his arm around Hazel and said, "Come on dear, let's get you back to the house. I'll fix us something to eat and you can sit and rest for a little bit." As they walked up the path toward the house Hazel wanted so badly to talk to her daddy about Matthew, but she just couldn't make herself.

CHAPTER 10

DINNER WITH THE PREACHER

Robert and Irene had been so busy trying to find the right furniture and set up their apartment that they had run out of time to get or fix anything to take to dinner. They had been told not to worry about it, but they hated to go empty handed to the Lands house.

As it turned out they didn't need to bring anything, there was more food than you could imagine. Irene thought that there it would be just the four of them, but the table was set for eight. "Well kids, come on in and make yourself at home." Said Mr. Lands. "I hope you don't mind, but we invited our pastor and his wife over as well. They have two of the sweetest kids you will ever meet. You are going to love those girls. One of them had polio and has a difficult time at some things, but she doesn't let it stop her. Her name is Penelope, of course we call her Penny for short, she is four, her sister's name is Lucille and she goes by Lucy, and she is five. Our Pastor's wife is a wonderful lady, her name is Hallie and our Pastor's name is Edward. He is a fiery young fellow. I'm looking forward for you meeting them." He said without so much as taking a breath. "Well we are looking forward to meeting them as well. Thank you for inviting us over and for helping with the furniture." Said Robert. Irene looked to Mrs. Lands and offered to help set the table and apologized at least a dozen times for not bringing anything for dinner.

At about 5:30 the Pastor and his family arrived and the men went into the living room to sit and "talk shop" as Walter Lands said. What they really talked about was a whole lot of nothing from what Irene could overhear. Irene was busy getting to know Penny and Lucy, whether she liked it or not. It's not that she didn't like the little girls, it was more the fact that she had spent the last couple of years with Roberts little brother's and was a little burned out, she supposed.

Just as Mr. Land's had said, Penny was so cute and hard not to love, she walked with a terrible limp, but it never seemed to slow her down. Irene was very impressed with the pastor's wife and was surprised to find that she had a lot in common with her. Of course, Mrs. Lands invited her to church on the following day. Irene politely made up an excuse as to why that was not possible, but said, maybe next week. She was absolutely certain that something would come up next week as well. None-the-less she enjoyed talking with Sister Nelson, who was quick to tell Irene to call her Hallie. They put the final touches on dinner and called the men in to the dining room.

When they all were seated, Robert picked up his fork to begin to eat when he noticed everyone, except Irene had bowed their heads and were getting ready to say grace. He put his fork down quickly and he and Irene bowed their heads, although neither one closed their eyes. She looked over at him about half way through the mini sermonette and he just smiled at her and winked.

Finally Walter Lands said amen and everyone began to pass the food around. Robert had already placed a spoon full of mashed potatoes on his plate and he passed the bowl around to the others. He hadn't realized how hungry he was until now, his stomach was growling which caused the little girls to giggle. "Stop that girls, that's not nice." "I'm sorry sir." Said Hallie. "Oh that's fine, my stomach was just gnawing at my back bone." Robert replied, somewhat nervously. "It's been a very long day and Irene and I just never seemed to take time to eat. With all of the excitement of the day and then trying to get the furniture in and set up a little in the apartment." He said.

"Boy wasn't that terrible about the little Johnson boy?" Said pastor Nelson. "It sure was." replied Mrs. Lands. "Those children were so small, can you just imagine how terrible that family must be doing." She continued. "I appreciate you all allowing us to have a prayer meeting over at the store, I mean church, today. I really felt like we needed to lift that family up in prayer." Said Pastor Nelson.

"Did they attend your church Rev. Nelson?" Asked Irene. "No ma'am, and please call me Paul. They don't attend, but I have done some work with the father, I have been trying to get him to come. I just hope that this doesn't make him bitter at God." He said. "We just really need to rally around them at this time." Said Hallie. They all just nodded and Mr. Lands quickly added, "You know, a person never really knows how much time they have in this ole world. It pays to be ready doesn't it Robert?"

Robert nearly choked on the piece of chicken that he was swallowing and looked over at Walter Lands in an attempt to make it look like he knew what they were talking about. "Oh yeah, it sure does." Robert said, although he wasn't even sure what 'it' was. "Yes sir, one minute your here and the next minute you are standing before God. That's a sobering thought isn't it pastor?" Walter said. "Well, the scripture declares in the book of Hebrews the ninth chapter and verse 27, 'It is appointed unto man once to die and after this the judgment.' Pastor Nelson continued. "It doesn't seem right that a child should die and wicked men live, but one thing is for sure, that baby is in heaven awaiting the glorious resurrection and when that day comes, those parents can see their child again. If they make things right with God that is."

By this time Robert was having a hard time swallowing his food. This conversation or that chicken wasn't settling too well. He looked over at Irene to see if she was as fidgety as he was and, for sure she was. They had never been around preachers and it seemed that they were doing everything except for receiving a collection. He actually wondered if that wasn't next. Irene tried to ask the girls a question about baby dolls and such, she was trying anything to change the discussion from death and dying and God.

Quite honestly she hadn't come to dinner to get preached at and she was a little resentful. She tried to busy herself so that her aggravation wouldn't show. She hated to think such a thing, but she was relieved when Penny poured a glass of tea on herself. At least for a few minutes it would distract everyone from the deep conversation.

Her and Robert ate as quickly as possible and began looking for a way to excuse themselves. They were in a hurry to get back to the apartment, with all of the new furniture; they just had to get the place cleaned up. At least that was the story they told and it seemed plausible howbeit hugely exaggerated.

Once they had politely visited for a little while longer and Irene helped wash the dishes, they said goodbye and made as fast of an exit as possible. When they were a safe distance from the house, they looked at each other and simultaneously said, "Oh Lord!" "Wasn't that uncomfortable?" Asked Irene. "Yes!" Said Robert. "I thought they were going to receive an offering, after all of that preaching. I'm sure glad you got us out of going to church with them tomorrow. I don't think I need any more church, at least not after tonight."

They picked up their stride and joined hands as they walked back toward the apartment. "Robert," Irene said inquisitively, "Do you think there really is a heaven?" "What?" Said Robert. "Are you seriously going to start that conversation up again?" He quipped. "I would rather not think anymore about that tonight, as a matter of fact, I don't think I want to for a long time to come." Robert said with a sense of aggravation, although he tried to keep it from showing. It didn't work.

"There is no need to get testy with me over it Robert. I just wondered whether that little baby went to heaven like the preacher said?" She asked, as she let go of his hand, clearly upset with the response that she had received. "Oh Irene, I don't know whether there's a heaven and if there is I am sure that baby is there and anyway, I didn't mean to be upset. I'm sorry for being short with you." Robert said, as he reached for her hand again. They walked on back to the apartment without saying anything else to each other. Their minds were in a whirl.

CHAPTER 11

THE DATE

"You are not my Mother!" Hazel screamed! "Quit trying to act like you are! If I want to go out with Matthew Thompson, I can. I am 18 years old and I don't need you telling me who I can and can't date!" In truth she wasn't 18, she was barely 17 but that didn't matter at least not to her. "At least I didn't get married when I was 13," she exclaimed. If her dad would have been home on that Saturday morning he would likely have punished her for those word's, but he was out running the dogs with Robert. "How dare you! How dare you scream at me," Irene responded. "Me getting married at 15 may have not been the smartest thing that I have ever done, but Robert and I have done very well together."

Irene continued, "You, on the other hand, are wanting to date someone who is nearly 10 years older than you and worse than that, he spends most of his time running moon shine. Don't you dare speak to me in that tone!" Irene shouted. "Matthew Thompson is trouble and everyone sees that but you," She continued. "If daddy knew that you were even considering going out with that man it would kill him." In fact her daddy didn't know and honestly, she didn't know how Irene knew. Regardless of how she had found out that Hazel was contemplating a date with Matthew, it didn't matter. She was going on that date and the fact that Irene was so against it, was all the more reason to proceed. "Don't you dare tell Daddy!" Hazel retorted. "You know that I would never do anything that would hurt him, let alone kill him."

That had been true all of her life. She was Oliver Trammels" baby girl and the two were inseparable. "You are the one that hurt daddy! You are the one that moved off and broke his heart." Hazel knew that she was exaggerating, but if Irene wanted to use daddy as a weapon against her, then she was all the more willing to turn that weapon right back at her sister. "You left him when you were 15 years old and you are going to judge me?" Hazel said. "I am going out with Matthew and you can't stop me." With that Hazel ran out the back door and off toward the pond. Oh how she had wished that Irene would have stopped her, how she wished a thousand times over that someone would have stopped her from making that horrible decision. It was a decision that would cause more grief than she could have ever imagined.

When Hazel got to the pond, she climbed up onto the low-lying limb of the old willow tree that had been as much a part of her life as anything or anyone else. This was where she would go when she just needed to get away. It's where she went when something was troubling her or she just needed a place to cry. On that Saturday morning Hazel was more troubled than ever.

She was about to make the biggest decision of her life and although everything about it seemed so wrong, she was determined that she was going to meet Matthew Thompson no matter what her sister or anyone else thought about it. Matthew was a mystical guy in some ways. She knew nothing about him. She had no idea where he lived or worked. He drove a neat car, it was a hotrod and Matthew always drove fast. There was no question that he was a good looking and popular man, even if his popularity was for all of the wrong reasons. He was tall and slender with thick black wavy hair and hazel eyes that sparkled with a mystique that was captivating. They had really never talked much, but he had asked her out and she had said yes. Now there was no way that Irene was going to tell her what she could and couldn't do. Without another thought, Hazel headed back to the house.

Her and Irene never talked much after that, certainly not that day. Hazel went to her room and got ready for her date. As she walked out of the bedroom, Irene was waiting for her. "I won't tell daddy, but you had better be home before dark." She said emphatically. Hazel sneered at her sister and left without saying a word. She had already asked to use the truck and since Irene and Robert were going to be there her dad had said yes. He didn't ask her why she needed it or where she was going and she didn't offer any information. She drove toward town feeling a sense of anger and pride for having stood up for herself to her sister and yet she felt a tinge of guilt for the way she was sneaking around behind her daddy's back. "Anyway, we are just going for a drive!" She thought.

There, across the street from the market was Matthew. He was sitting on the hood of the car smoking a cigarette. She never knew that he smoked, but then again, she honestly knew nothing about him. As she got out and walked toward him, he took one more drag on the cigarette and then exhaled. It swirled above his head like a doughnut. He tossed the cigarette into the street and smashed it with his boot. Matthew reached out for Hazel's hand. Her daddy had never smoked and certainly would not condone it, but then again, there was nothing about Matthew that Oliver would condone. Hazel's heart was pounding so loudly in her ears that she could hear it.

She thought for a moment that it would be best just to call it all off and yet she just couldn't seem to muster up the strength to do it. She wasn't going to give her sister the pleasure of being right, besides, what would it hurt? It was just a drive and maybe something to eat, she mused. Her mind was racing and she just couldn't seem to shake the nervousness and the feelings of betrayal. Her dad would be so upset if he found out. Although Hazel was now 17 years old or as she liked to think, almost 18, she was still innocent enough to care what her daddy thought. She had never dated anyone and really had never had an interest in dating. She was sometimes repulsed by the idea, probably because of the way Irene had been about Robert. Either way, she stood there, trying to decide whether or not she should take the hand of this man, whom she hardly knew, but she did.

Matthew escorted her to the car, opened the door for her and closed the door behind her. She learned very quickly that he loved to drive fast and he seemed to live as fast as he drove. The tires squalled as the car slid sideways for a moment before he straightened it back out and gave it gas. As the car slid so did she and before she knew what was happening, she was over against him and holding tightly to his arm. Both the car and their relationship were going way too fast. The next few hours were a blur, but one thing was certain, things had gone too far. By the time they had arrived back in town, it was nearly eleven o'clock and the only vehicle left on the street was her daddy's truck. Sitting there on the tailgate of the truck was her dad.

CHAPTER 12

INNOCENCE LOST

As Matthew pulled in across the street, Hazel saw her father wiping tears from his face. She didn't know how long he had been there, but he was clearly worried and broken hearted. He walked over to the car and opened the door for his daughter, took her by the hand as she straightened her wrinkled clothes. He started to say something to Matthew, but caught himself.

They got in the truck and Oliver drove home. Not a word was spoken, nothing was said, and nothing could be said. When they got to the house she noticed that Irene and Robert were already gone and thought to ask why, but she dare not speak. They walked somberly toward the house and once inside she went toward her room and turned to say something to her daddy, but what was she to say? "Good night daddy, I love you." The words just naturally rolled off of her lips. She had said the same thing every night since she had learned how to talk. This time, instead of a smile and a kiss on the forehead, she saw tears. It was clear that he wanted to tell her what he had always said, "I love you my beautiful girl!" But those words just couldn't form in his broken heart.

Hazel stepped into her room and shut the door. She crumpled to the floor and sat there all night long, listening to the deep sobs of her daddy on the other side of the wall. What had she done? How could she do this to him? Worse yet was what she had done to herself. In the heat of passion she had lost her innocence and now there was so much more to think about than just her daddy. After that moment Matthew never really said anything, he just drove her back to town and there was her dad. Why didn't he try to say something to her father? Why didn't he say anything to her? Why had she put herself in such a place as that in the first place and now, what if...what if she was pregnant? The answer came soon enough.

As Matthew sped out of Purdin that night, he couldn't help but feel a little nervous. Not because of what had happened between him and Hazel, that was no big deal to him, no his feelings came from the look that her dad had give him. He remembered that look all too well. With that he stepped on the pedal and shot down the winding road and back toward Inez. No matter what he did he just couldn't shake that stare. It literally caused him to shiver as though a cool breeze blew across his neck. "This is crazy, I'm not afraid of that ole man," He thought aloud. "Besides, he doesn't even know who I am or anything else about me," Matthew continued.

The truth was though, he was afraid and the more he thought about it, the more scared he became. He chalked it up to the beating that he had taken from Helen's dad a few weeks earlier. Matthew shot by a little shack that sat on the side of the road, some of the locals called it a night club, but it was really just a ran down hole in the road where you could get a stiff drink and occasionally listen to a bunch of drunks howling at the moon.

He locked the car up and spun around in the middle of the road and headed back to get something to clear his head. Before the car even fully stopped he could hear the loud cursing that was commonplace in dives like this. He jumped out of the car and stepped inside, the smoke was so thick there was no way that anyone could have seen him and if they did, it wasn't likely that they would have paid attention. Matthew ordered a whiskey and guzzled it down as fast as he could. "Surely this will get my mind off of that old man," he thought. Just as he started to order another drink, through the thick smoke, Matthew caught a glimpse of a man that made his heart stop! The fear he had been dealing before that shot of whiskey was now multiplied a thousand times over. Sitting about 20 feet to his left was Helen's dad, the same guy that had left him on the side of the road half dead. He had warned Matthew to stay away and now he had better figure out how to get away. Just then someone on the other side of the man began cussing Helen's dad. Before Matthew knew what had happened, the two of them tore into each other. This was the diversion he had been looking for; he quickly laid a half a dollar on the bar and hurriedly moved to the door and slipped back out into the darkness.

All he could think about was getting back to Inez and

as far away from Purdin as he could get. It wasn't particularly hot that night but he found himself soaked with sweat. A few minutes later he reached the edge of town and took his favorite back road toward his house. As he coasted to a stop and killed the engine, he thought briefly about just going into the house and going to bed, but instead he turned toward the barn.

Normally getting paid was no big deal, there would be an envelope waiting for him, tucked under an old water bucket just inside the door. "I'll go ahead and get my money and then I'm going to get some sleep," Matthew said to himself. Unfortunately for him, this wasn't going to be a normal night. When he stepped inside the door of the barn and reached for the bucket he felt the thud of a pipe or something across the back of his head. He crumpled to the floor and was out cold.

CHAPTER 13

THE LONG AWAITED TALK

Oliver's house had been quiet, eerily quiet ever since that night in late April. Hazel had noticed some nausea and was too afraid to think what that might mean. She hadn't heard from Matthew and honestly, that was the last thing on her mind. She had finished school a few weeks later and although only a junior in school it would be her last year. By the time summer rolled around, Hazel knew that her greatest fear was now a reality. She was experiencing morning sickness and nausea nearly everyday. Hazel knew that she was pregnant and that it was going to be, a very long summer.

One of the most difficult things facing her was trying to figure out how to tell her dad. She was certain that he knew already. He had tried to offer her help, but things were so awkward between them. Her pregnancy was the preverbal "elephant in the room," everyone saw it, but no one wanted to talk about it. Not a word had been spoken about that night; actually, they never spoke much at all. He loved her and she knew that, but she also knew that she had broken his heart in a way that a million words could never heal.

Oliver had been out much later than normal and Hazel was beginning to worry. It wasn't like him to be gone so long. Oliver worked as an officer for the forestry department; it was a very good job. He was one of the few men in the area not working at the coalmines. His job in forestry management afforded him some decent hours and good pay. It had also allowed for some much-needed flexibilities to raise two daughters alone.

He was almost always home before dark. Now Hazel found herself pacing the floor of the small three-bedroom house and going from window to window looking for her dad's truck to pull in. Hazel feared the worst and what made the thought of something happening to her dad even more difficult was the divide that now separated them.

It was nearly 10:00 pm when the lights of Oliver's truck shined through the window in the living room. Hazel breathed a sigh of relief. Perhaps it was too late to tell her daddy the news? Maybe it would be best to just go to bed and hope for a better day to tell her dad about her pregnancy? Hazel knew that she couldn't wait another day so she took a deep breath to slow her heartbeat and waited. "What is taking daddy so long?" She asked herself. "Why is he just standing there by the truck and not coming inside?" Again Hazel thought she should forgo the conversation, but just then the door opened and Oliver stepped inside. His face was pale, his shirt was soaked from sweat and his eyes were staring wildly.

"Daddy!" Hazel cried. "Daddy, what is wrong? Are you alright?" She asked. She had never seen him look like that. "Daddy, are you okay?" She asked again, but Oliver never answered, he just stood there. Hazel reached for his hand and asked him to sit down. "Please daddy, let me get you a glass of water." She said. Oliver sauntered over to his chair and sat down. "Do you need me to go get Mr. Gavin?" Asked Hazel. Mr. Gavin was their neighbor and she knew that he had been a medic in the Army and thought surely he could help. "No, no I'll be fine." Oliver finally said.

"What is wrong daddy, are you hurting, did you have an accident?" Hazel asked. She was grasping for any information, which might explain the shape that her dad was in. Oliver sat there for a moment, reached in to his back pocket and pulled a handkerchief out and wiped his brow. Hazel hurried to the bathroom and returned with a dampened washcloth and handed it to her dad. He wiped his face and neck and took a drink of water from the glass she had brought him.

"Hazel, honey, I need to talk to you about something." Oliver finally said. "What is it daddy?" She replied. "This isn't easy for me and I don't quite know where to start, but something is troubling me and I have to ask you a very hard question. Are you...?" His voice trailed and his lips quivered. He took another drink of water and steadied himself and finished his question. "Are you pregnant?"

Hazel could not believe what she was hearing, it was the conversation she had planned to have with her daddy, but she could never have imagined that he would be the one initiating it. She had been rehearsing her approach to this very difficult subject all evening and was completely taken aback.

Since the night when she snuck out with Matthew, her relationship with her dad had become strained and there had been very little communication between them. She had tried to hide the sickness to the best of her ability and yet down deep inside she knew that her dad was no dummy. Hazel couldn't help herself, her emotions got the best of her and she burst into tears. "Daddy!" She began, "I am so sorry! I didn't mean to hurt you and I..." The words just seemed stuck in her throat. "Daddy, I, I am pregnant." All of the emotions that she had been bottling up came flooding out. Hazel fell to the floor by her dads' feet and began sobbing uncontrollably.

Oliver put his hand on her shoulder and tried to find the words to say to take away the heartache that his little girl felt, but the words just wouldn't come out. Hazel was crumpled up in a ball at his feet and he couldn't formulate the words to help her. He sat there and patted her on the shoulder as his mind began to wonder back to the drive he had taken that afternoon.

He couldn't seem to shake Matthews face from his mind. He had come so close to dropping the bum dead in his tracks, but couldn't make himself do it. Now he wished that he had. "No one would have ever known." He had reasoned within himself. Instead of pulling the trigger Oliver watched

Matthew get out of his car and walked across the yard. This was his chance and in spite of all of his planning and contemplation, he simply couldn't do it.

Oliver was shaking uncontrollably as a cool breeze swept over his sweat-drenched shirt. He had been sitting there in the wooded area that was no more than a hundred yards from Matthews house for more than three hours. He had rehearsed the plans a thousand times and now, now when push came to shove, he couldn't fire the shot.

The Savage 99 had been given to him as a gift and was the most accurate gun that Oliver had, but accuracy meant nothing if you couldn't pull the trigger. He sat there shaking in the night air, trying to pull himself together. Finally, Oliver stood to his feet, crouched as low as he could so as not to be seen and slipped away from the tree line and back toward his truck. He knew that he hadn't been seen and yet he was scared to death. The short walk back to his truck seemed much longer than it was. The moon was shining bright and Oliver moved slowly and deliberately through the woods.

As he arrived at his truck, Oliver quietly opened the door and slid the rifle across the seat. He reached into his pocket and pulled out his keys, sat down in the drivers seat and turned the ignition. The engine fired up and Oliver drove as quickly as he could out of Inez and back toward home. The drive home was filled with hard, raw emotions as Oliver at one moment breathed a sigh of relief that he had not killed Matthew, and the next moment he berated himself for not having the guts to do what he felt needed to be done. He drove with the windows down and the cold night air washed over his body.

"Why do I have to face this alone?" Oliver shouted out loud. He knew that if Anna was still alive, she would never have allowed him to do what he had nearly done, but he surmised, "Someone needs to take care of Matthew Thompson!" He spoke as though he were arguing with his wife. He drove in silence the rest of the way home.

When he arrived at home he was surprised to see the lights on. He had figured that Hazel would have already gone to bed and that he would be able to slip in and put the rifle back under the bed where he kept it and no one would be the wiser. Oliver shut off the engine and just sat there, staring across the moon lit field. Finally he shut the truck off, opened the door, stepped out of the truck pulled the seat forward and slipped the rifle behind the seat.

Oliver didn't realize how disheveled he looked, and certainly never dreamed that he would even think of asking his little girl if she was pregnant, he had known the answer before he had asked, he wasn't a fool. Anna had been pregnant with three children and although she lost one early on in her pregnancy, she still experienced all of the morning sickness. It was the same sickness that he had watched Hazel deal with for the past few weeks.

MOMENTS-THE STORY OF GIL AND MACEY

Oliver couldn't muster up the words to console his daughter who now knelt in front of his chair. So he just ran his fingers through her hair and occasionally would say, "It's going to be okay honey!" He didn't know for sure if it would be, but he tried to sound convincing.

Hazel finally looked up at her dad and told him again how sorry she was for the embarrassment that she had brought upon him. He tried again to assure her that everything would be okay. Hazel wiped her eyes and stood to her feet. Oliver stood as well and they hugged. "We are going to make it through this sweetheart, don't you worry." Hazel looked her dad in the eyes and told him again, how sorry she was and then turned toward her room. Oliver wanted to tell her how much he loved her and yet, all that he could do was watch her go into her room and shut the door.

He sat back down in the chair as his mind began to rehearse the day's events and just how close he had come to firing that shot. Some time later, Oliver slipped quietly across the floor and out to the truck to retrieve his rifle. He came back inside and into his room where he tucked the gun under his bed, sat down on the edge of the bed and began to cry.

Over the next few weeks, Oliver took every available opportunity to work overtime. By the time fall rolled around life had nearly returned to normal, whatever that meant.

Hazel was unable to go to school for her senior year. She was as big as a barrel and had nothing to wear; besides, she was too embarrassed to even think about going to school and facing her friends. It was hard enough dealing with the guilt of hurting her father and betraying his trust. For the most part Hazel had spent all summer and fall in hiding. She had shamed him and his good name.

Finally in October, they had that talk, if you could call it a talk. One night after supper, Hazel put away the dishes and walked into the living room where her dad was sitting in his easy chair reading the paper. She stood there for a moment and then walked slowly across the room where he sat. After a few moments He looked over the paper and saw her standing there, staring at him from behind the paper. He saw her, not as a pregnant woman who had shamed him, but as his little girl.

Oliver laid the paper down, and motioned to Hazel to come and sit on his knee. Nothing was said for a long time. She just sat there with her arms around her daddy and his around her and they wept together. After a while, he looked at her and said, "Sweetheart, I love you and I forgive you for anything that you have done." Hazel tried to talk, but couldn't. She broke into tears. It seemed they would never stop, it felt like oceans were flowing out of her eyes. She wrapped her arms tightly around her daddy and just kept saying, "I love you daddy, and I am so sorry."

CHAPTER 14

THE NEXT ASSIGNMENT

It was much later when Matthew began to arouse. He was sitting in a dark musky room and it felt like a chain of some sort was wrapped around his waist. His hands were tied to the floor with a piece of wire or something, whatever it was seemed to be cutting into his wrist the more that he pulled against it. His eyes were blurry and the room was so dark that he could barely see anything. Before he could get his eyes adjusted to the what little bit of light was filtering through, he felt the sting of an open-handed and very hard slap across his face. Again he was hit, except this time it was more of a punch. "Who are you and what are you doing?" Matthew screamed. "Shut up and listen." The man shouted. "We will ask the questions, but not until we are ready." Matthew retorted, "Do you mean that you are just going to beat me to death and then ask me questions when I'm dead."

He was in no place to be smart with anyone, but he had to attempt to talk some sense into these people, whoever they were. It didn't work. The man put his boot squarely in Matthew's chest. Every ounce of air shot out of his lungs and he felt like he was going to pass out. Just then the man grabbed him by his ear and pulled so hard he thought it would come off. Matthew screamed. "I want you to listen to me punk! I don't know if you know who you are messing with, but I want you to understand something, we didn't mess around with your boss and we ain't messing with you either. He chose not to cooperate and now he's floating down the river so go ahead and get smart with me and you are going to find yourself in the same place.

Jim owed us some money and thought he could fool us, so now Jim is gone. The question you need to ask yourself is, do you want to live or die? The only reason I haven't already taken care of you is because I am not sure how much you know or if you are just a runner. If you are a runner and nothing more, you may be useful." "I'm telling you I don't know anything, I never saw anybody and I never asked questions. They would tell me where to go and I went where I was told. I would deliver the stuff and then come back to the shop; my pay was always under the bucket by the door. I'd get it and get out. I promise you, I don't know nothing!" Matthew said as desperately as he could muster. It was true, he knew nothing about the workings of the operation, they just knew that he was a good driver and he had proven himself to them. He had never shorted them anything other than an occasional jug for his dad.

He had no intention of meeting the same fate of those for whom he had been working. "Listen to me please, I'm good at what I do and I don't care if it's for you or whoever, just let me do the running and let me live." He said. About that time another guy stepped out of the shadows in the back of the room.

He was a heavyset guy, probably no more than 5'8" but very heavy. He had an unlit cigar stuck out the side of his mouth and he moved toward Matthew as he chewed on the ole stogy. "I told you he was straight." Said the man. "Listen, boy, we had some problems with some missing money and we don't have time for that. It was either you or Jim and there wasn't a lot of time to try to sort it out.

We had decided to kill two birds with one stone, if you know what I mean. Lucky for you, I believe you. That's not to say that I'm totally convinced, but I'm willing to give you a chance to prove yourself to my friends and me. You had better listen really good to me boy, if I ever feel like you are dirty dealing or messing with me, there won't be any discussions. You see Clarence here? He likes to inflict pain. Actually he would rather do more than inflict pain and you better be thankful that me and the others gave you a chance to explain yourself."

"Mister, I just want to do my job and get my money, I ain't gonna cheat anyone. Whatever anyone else did ain't got anything to do with me." Replied Matthew. The Heavy set man looked at Clarence and told him to let Matthew loose. Clarence grunted, but did as he was told. While the chain was being taken off of Matthew the heavyset man said, "Jim found out the hard way what happens when you double cross me. I'm warning you this one time, don't even think about it. The next time, Clarence won't think twice about breaking you in a million pieces. Are we clear?" Asked the man. "Yes sir! Perfectly, but can I ask you a question? Am I going to get paid for my last run?" Matthew asked.

The man reached in his back pocket and handed an envelope to him. "From now on, you don't come by the shop when you are in town. We will get the money to you. You just check in the alley behind your house. There is a yellow sign nailed onto the side of the shed. Your money will be there. As far as the car goes, we will take it and load it when we are ready for a run, we'll back it in to the driveway and leave directions under the dash telling you where to go. You will drop the stuff and bring the cash back and exchange it for your pay. If there is a penny missing you are a dead man. You got that?" He asked Matthew. "Yes, yes I got it." Matthew replied. "Now get out of here." The man demanded.

Matthew didn't know what to think. He had never seen Clarence or the other guy, come to think of it, he had never really had any communication with anyone. He always tried to move in and get the stuff and get out without much conversation. He knew better than mess with them.

As Matthew walked toward the spot where he had left his car he couldn't help but wonder who these guys were. He was up to his neck in the 'company' and he didn't have a clue who or what, the 'company' was. He wandered what had really become of Jim and why they had let him live. He surmised that they needed him. If the need for a good driver was the reason for him still being alive, he was quite thankful for that. There wasn't a better driver in the state than Matthew. He also knew that he had better mind himself and be very careful, because one thing was certain, he never wanted to experience Clarence again.

His head hurt and it felt like his chest was bruising something terrible. He thought aloud, "Why did he have to nearly pull my ear off?" His car was gone from its spot and Matthew understood this to mean, they were getting it ready for another run. It also meant that if he was going to get any rest, he better do it fast. He went into his room and collapsed on the bed and quickly drifted off to sleep. It had been a long hard run! The fatigue and the powerful blow to the head was more than enough to help him want to forget it all.

CHAPTER 15

RUNNING OUT OF LUCK

Matthew woke up to an excruciating headache. The light that was beaming through the bedroom window was adding to his discomfort. The room was stifling hot and he knew that it was afternoon because that was the only time the sunlight came through that window. He struggled to see the clock and when he did he could hardly believe what he was seeing. The clock showed that it was nearly 4:00. What day was this and how long had he slept. Had he dreamed all of this stuff up?

If it weren't for the excruciating headache, he would have thought it all a bad dream. After a few minutes Matthew staggered toward the window. He looked up toward the garage to see if his car was where they said it would be. True enough, it was right where he had be been told it would be. It was backed in to the spot along side of the garage. Suddenly the seriousness of the moment hit him. If the car is there then there is a run to be made and if there is a run to be made then there is a deadline. "If I'm late for the run, then I'm in serious trouble." Matthew thought out loud.

He understood the reason for those who were running the operation to want to stay in the dark, but he had been use to setting his own schedule to some extent. If he wanted to make an extra run he had been able to, but now he had no idea how things were going to play out. He was anxious to see where his next stop would be. Matthew quickly washed and shaved and headed to the car. He decided it would be a good idea to use more caution as he approached the car.

He looked around to make sure that he wasn't being watched, and slid in behind the steering wheel. He reached up under the dash to his right, just under the temperature gauge and felt until he found a folded paper. "You are already gassed up, go to Claremont, turn on county road 112 go 1 mile to the driveway across from the old church. The barn is on the right a half a mile ahead. You have to be there by six. They will gas your car up when you are done." He looked at his watch and realized that he had a little less than two hours. He knew that was plenty of time if nothing went wrong, but he also knew the six gallons of gas that his car held would not get him there. Which meant, he would have to find a station along the way.

He had never delivered anything to this place and he had no time to waste. If he got lost or turned around, he could easily be late. Matthew put the car in gear and sped out of town headed toward Claremont. To get there he would have to go through Purdin and Bromley. If he didn't push it too hard he should be able to make it to Bromley before he gassed up and then on the way back he could stop at Purdin. "No," he was practically yelling at himself, "There is no way

I am going near that town!"

Again Matthew found himself nervous, very nervous. He could not run the risk of being seen by the wrong people in Purdin. Helen's father was no one to mess with and the fact that he had friends who were working for the sheriffs department, added to his cautious attitude. The last place he wanted to be was anywhere near Hazels dad either but he also knew better than to miss his appointment because then he would have to deal with Clarence. He wasted no time as he passed through the outer part of Purdin and quickly sped on to Bromley. The station on the edge of town was closed and Matthew knew that he was running on fumes. He had only been to Bromley a couple of times and couldn't remember whether there was another station in town. He hoped against hope there may be one close enough to keep him from running out of gas, unfortunately for Matthew, there wasn't.

The car sputtered and died, and he quickly stepped on the clutch to get as much distance as possible in hopes that he may get closer to a station. He could little afford to be late for his appointment and definitely did not need to draw any attention from anyone, considering the load he was carrying. The car slowed and came to a stop on the side of highway 19 that meandered through the little town along side the train tracks. It was a Monday evening and, although there were quite a few people out and about, either they didn't realize that he was broke down or too self absorbed to offer assistance. It really didn't matter anyway, what mattered is that he had an appointment and it didn't appear that he was going to make it. Matthew was mad at himself, but more than that, he was worried about giving Clarence a reason to be mad.

How could he have let this happen? Matthew scanned the houses on either side of Highway 19 to see if there was someone who may be outside, or maybe a shed or garage where he could find a gas can. There on the right side of the road just across the track he watched as an elderly gentleman drove his truck into the garage on the side of house. Matthew quickly ran toward the house and as the gentleman stepped out around the corner Matthew met him by the porch. "Good evening sir, I didn't mean to startle you, but I ran out of gas and was wondering if you have any that I might buy from you?" Matthew said. Just then he noticed the star on his left shirt pocket. Of all of the people that he could have chosen to ask for help he had to choose a deputy. "Young man," said the deputy, "that's a good way to get yourself shot!" Although he was up in years, it was obvious to Matthew that the deputy was still in pretty good shape. "I'm really sorry sir." Said Matthew. "I was traveling through on my way to Claremont to see my grandmother who is ill. They told me that she may not make it much longer and I didn't want something to happen to her without me getting to see her. I thought I had enough gas to get me there, but unfortunately I was wrong. If you could help me I would really appreciate it. If Gram dies before I get there, I'll never forgive myself."

It was all a lie but it was much better than telling the lawman the truth. What was he supposed to say, "I'm hauling shine and my tank only holds six gallons of gas because most of the tank is blocked off for the stuff?" Matthew sniffed as though he were trying to choke back a tear. "Well now son, I don't want you to miss getting to see your grandma. Let's see if there is any gas here in the shed. By the way, what's your grandma's name? I have some family over in Claremont, I may know her." Said the deputy. Matthew stumbled over a tree root that was sticking up out of the ground and nearly fell on his face. He was glad he did because he couldn't think of a name to give the deputy and his fall gave him a few extra moments to come up with one.

"Mueller, sir." Matthew said, hoping that wasn't the deputy's name. "Mueller huh?" Said the deputy. "I don't know any Mueller's over in Claremont." He continued. "What's her first name?" Matthew thought quickly and then responded, "Bertha sir, Bertha Mueller. She hasn't lived there long, um, she was originally from up in Hagerty." His answer seemed to work because the officer never asked anymore about her. "Well, let's see here, this can has a gallon or so in it but I'm not sure if its regular or Ethel." Said the deputy. "Either one will do." Said Matthew as he quickly reached of the can of gas. "I'll run over and pour it in the tank and bring your gas can right back sir."

Before the officer could say anything Matthew had the can in his hand and was sprinting toward the car. He checked the tracks to make sure the train wasn't coming and then shot across the tracks to his car. He poured most of the gas in the car and kept just enough in the can to prime the car. He popped the hood and poured the rest of the gas in the carburetor, laid the can on the ground jumped in the car and hit the key. To his delight the car roared to life. Matthew left the car idling and ran as fast as he could to the waiting deputy. "Here you go sir, here is your can and here is dollar for the gas." He said. "No son, you keep that dollar, you just get on over and see your grandma before something happens to her." Said the officer.

With no argument Matthew quickly stuffed the dollar back in his pocket said thanks and rushed to the car. "By the way son, you might want to get those tires checked, they seem to be a little low on air." Said the deputy. In truth they weren't low on air and Matthew knew it, the reason the tires seemed to be squatting was because of the load that was in the car but Matthew decided to play along. "Oh yes sir, I guess I better, uh, thank you sir and thank you for the gas." He said. Just about a half a mile down the road, at the edge of Bromley, Matthew saw a gas station. He pulled in and was getting ready to pump the gas himself when the attendant ran out to the car. "Here you go sir. Let me pump that for you." He said, as he grabbed the pump handle out of his hand. "We pride our self in being the fastest station in Purdin, but that's not too hard since Barton's went out of business.

I was noticing that your car seems to be squatting a little in the back, do you want me to check and see if something is wrong with the springs?" Said the attendant. "No!" Matthew yelled back. "I don't need you to check my springs, just pump the gas and get out of the way so I can get on the road." The man was clearly rattled and did exactly what he was told to do. "I'm sorry buddy, I didn't mean to roil you. I was just trying to help. If you don't want me to check it out for you that is your business, but I'm telling you something is wrong with the back suspension. If Mr. Alexander, our mechanic was here he could tell you right off what's wrong with it.

He is probably the best mechanic I have ever met, he can hear a car and tell you exactly what is wrong without even lifting the hood." The attendant said as he topped off the tank and screwed the cap back on. As he did Matthew handed him three dollars, which was more than he owed but he had wasted enough time and knew that if he gave this guy another minute he would take twenty. "Keep the change bud." Matthew said. "Hey, wait a minute, I'm supposed to wash the windows and check the oil too..." The attendant was still talking as Matthew jumped in the car and sped away as quickly as possible. He now had less than a half an hour to get

MOMENTS-THE STORY OF GIL AND MACEY

to his place.

Highway 42 was much more curvy than 19 had been and as Matthew navigated around one of the 90 degree curves he felt the rear end of the car kick out a little. "Man this thing must be loaded down a lot more than normal." He thought. As he neared Claremont he noticed the car doing it again but this time it wasn't on a curve. Matthew let up on the gas and thought of stopping to check it out but then realized there was no time for that. He gave it the gas and within a few minutes saw the old church and the county road that led to his drop spot.

He turned on the old gravel road and there about a half mile ahead he saw an old dirt lane. When he turned on to the lane he heard a pop in the back end of the car. He was certain that something had broken but this was no time to brake down and no place to brake down. He drove slowly down the lane until he saw the old barn on the left. As Matthew approached the barn, a man with a shotgun met him. He waved his right arm and Matthew brought the car to a stop. "Pull around back and into the big door on the other side. Stay in the car and don't move until we tell you.

When we are done, you will back out and go back the way you came." He said. Matthew did exactly as he was told and in about 43 minutes he was told to back up and get going. As he stepped on the gas at the end of the lane and turned back on to the gravel again the car shifted. Matthew had thought about going on into Claremont to get someone to check his car but

111

then remembered the rattle box of an attendant back at Bromley and decided to find out if they really did have a good mechanic. The car was loose and every time he hit a curve it felt like the car was going to shift off of the frame.

Matthew crippled his car into the station and before he could get it shut off, the attendant met him. "Whoa, now something is really messed up sir. I told you to let me get it checked when you came through earlier. I knew there was something wrong with it. Good for you though cause now Mr. Alexander is here and even though it's late, I'm sure he can get it going for you." Said the attendant. Without saying another word or waiting for a response from Matthew, he ran back into the building and came back a few moments later with an older gentleman whose hands were covered in grease. "I can tell you what's wrong with it by the way she's setting, my guess is, you got a broken leaf spring in the back."

The old fellow walked around the car and as he was kneeling down to look up under the rear end, Matthew heard him talking to himself, "Hmm, a 1940 Ford Coupe." Matthew didn't know if he was asking or telling him, but he answered him just the same. "Yes sir." Said Matthew. "Hmmm, well I'll be" he could hear the man muttering. "Son, it looks like someone has reinforced the springs on this thing." Said the man. "Can you fix it?" Asked Matthew. "Sure can. I might even have what I need in the back."

Before he knew it Mr. Alexander had the car jacked up and was underneath it. "It looks like you have had her worked on before?" He asked. "No sir." Said Matthew. "Well, someone has done some welding under here. It looks like a blind man did the welding. That gas tank is a mess, and these reinforced springs seem a little strange. Do you want me to drain it and fix this weld?" Said Mr. Alexander. "No, no, that won't be necessary, I forgot about that. I got it from a fella that was a shade tree mechanic and it is possible that he did some stuff to it. But, I uh, I don't need you to do any more than the spring." Said Matthew. "It sure is a mess under here buddy." Alexander continued. "I wouldn't trust this thing from here to Purdin. You know, I hate to say it son but something looks mighty suspicious about the way they got this tank rigged up. Who did you say you got it from?" "I don't remember his name, anyway, I just need you to fix the spring and when I get back home I'll take care of the rest," said Mathew.

He was fighting hard to not show how nervous he was, but wasn't sure it was working. If this guy was to look too close, he knew that he was going to be in trouble. While he really hadn't known how much alterations had been done, he knew enough to know that things were getting a little dicey right now. "Are you going to be able to get that spring replaced?" Asked Matthew? "I'm supposed to meet a girl over in Purdin this afternoon." He continued. Which was also a lie, there was no way he was going to be stopping at Purdin, not then or any other time if he had his way.

"Yeah, I just about have it, but I'm telling you this thing ain't safe to drive." Mr. Alexander replied. "I'll just have to take it easy." Said Matthew. With that the mechanic slid out from under the car and let it down from the jack. He reached over and grabbed a shop towel off of the shelf and briskly wiped his hands with it. "Young fellow, I have a brother who is a lawman over in Purdin and I think that he might like to have a look at this car. Whoever you bought this thing from was into something that could get him in a lot of trouble..." The mechanic wasn't done but Matthew cut him off. "Don't you worry buddy, I'm going to have myself a little talk with the ole guy, but right now, I really need to get going."

Mr. Alexander started to say something else, but instead he just wrote out a bill for Matthew for $17.00 and handed it to him. Matthew thought for a moment to complain about the cost of the repair, but decided he had better just pay it and get out of there. He reached in his pocket and pulled out his money and hurriedly paid the mechanic. "So, you say you are going to Purdin huh?" asked Alexander. "Well, actually I'm going through there. I have a date this evening and I'm going to be late if I don't get going. Thank you for fixing my spring and don't you think for a moment that I'm not going to get ahold of the guy I bought it from." Matthew said as he quickly got in the car. Without any hesitation, he started it up and waved goodbye as he put it in reverse and gave it the gas. He drove as quickly as he could down highway 19 toward Purdin and was as nervous as cat in a room full of rocking chairs. He found himself looking in the rear view mirror every other minute. What time he wasn't watching the road behind him he was watching every side road and drive along the way.

He tried as hard as possible to get by Purdin without being seen and all the while hoped that the car would hold together long enough to get him away from there. He was relieved that he hadn't heard anymore of the popping in the rear end, but couldn't help but wonder if the old car would get him back home. That mechanic was no dummy and the fact that he had a brother who was a lawman certainly added to Matthews concern. He had a tough time not letting his nerves get the best of him. He had no intention of hanging close to Purdin or at least not near town. He hit the gas, skipped first gear and felt the car slip sideways as he quickly steered into the skid and straightened the car out. The rear end still felt weird but he would have to worry about that later.

As he sped away from town he couldn't help but think about that night and about Hazel. Matthew was a player and whether it was running shine or chasing women, he was always on the move. He had spent most of the past few years seeing how much he could get by with and this girl was just another on a long list. She had meant no more to him than the shine that had been emptied from his tank a few hours earlier. There on the side of the road, Matthew did what he had done so many other times; he stole the innocence of a girl he never knew.

As they headed back in to town, neither of them had said a word. He could hear her crying and could see her wiping her eyes but all he could think of was getting back home without getting caught by a lawman. Somehow the thought of seeing a deputy faded from his mind as he remembered the look that he got from Hazel's father. He had tried not to make eye contact with him and was relieved when the old fellow just opened the door and the girl got out. She never looked back and that was fine. As Matthew started to pull away he glanced toward the guy. He had seen that look before, as a matter of fact it had happened in this very town. Helen's father looked at him like that before beating him half to death. Matthew floored the car and quickly sped off, he thought to himself, "I have got to put some distance between me and this town.

He had only gone about five miles when he felt the rear end of the car kick hard to the left. He wasn't sure what had happened but he knew that this was going to be bad. He struggled to keep it on the road, but it was a fight and he quickly realized, he wasn't going to win this fight. There was a truck heading straight toward him, it wasn't the truck drivers fault, when Matthew swerved he had pulled into the wrong lane. The driver cut his wheel, but it was too late.

Matthew felt the impact as he slammed into the side

of the truck. Produce flew everywhere as the truck kicked over on its side and Matthew spun wildly out of control. He fought with everything in him to keep the car from flipping or rolling. He had caught the back of the truck just behind the rear tire, just enough to cause the truck to roll. With some luck and skill, Matthew gained control of the car. It was in bad shape and he knew it. Not just from the impact with the truck but whatever had happened from underneath the car. As he looked back in his rearview mirror he could see the truck lying on its side. For a moment he thought to stop and check on the driver, but he knew better than risk it. This was no place to be stopping and there was no way he could risk someone getting their hands on that car.

The drive home was tough, he had only one headlight, and something broken on the rear end and his nerves were on edge. As he limped the old car into town and pulled in to the shed that he normally parked by, all that he could think of was getting out of sight and some much needed rest.

CHAPTER 16

SISTER IRENE

For Hazel the final three months of her pregnancy seemed to last three years. Her heart was so much lighter since her and her father had talked, but still she longed for a relationship with her sister. Irene and Robert would come on Fridays and generally stay until Sunday afternoon, but Irene and Hazel seldom talked. There was a wall between them and although Oliver tried to tear it down, it seemed as though there was no way to overcome the incredible differences between his daughters.

Thankfully when Irene was visiting, much of the conversation was about Salyersville and the apartment, it was all she ever talked about.

During the early parts of the pregnancy Hazel was able to avoid hearing about it, but as she got further along and too big to be able to get away, she was generally stuck listening to her sisters whining. "Daddy," She would say, "Those people are as sweet as can be, but they are really weird. They pray and sing so loud." She continued. "They have church on Wednesday nights, prayer on Friday, church on Sunday, not just morning mind you, but Sunday nights too. Let me tell you," she continued. "On top of that, they have had two revivals since we moved in."

Once Hazel asked, "What's a revival?" "Well let me

tell you." Irene bemoaned. "It's when crazy people get together and have church for endless hours while people who live upstairs try to figure out how to drown out the noise. I'm not even kidding. They can go for hours and hours. Am I telling the truth Robert?" She asked, although she never paused long enough to hear the answer. "The floor just shakes with the clapping and shouting." "Shouting?" asked Oliver.

"That's what they call it. One time Robert and me snuck to the top of the stairwell to see what the commotion was and you wouldn't believe it. There were people doing some kind of dance and others who were just hooting and hollering. One time I asked Mr. Lands, he's our landlord, I said, Mr. Lands, what is all of the commotion and he said," "Oh that is just people getting happy." She continued without breathing, "Well, the look on my face must have been something, because he quickly added, 'they are just shouting because Jesus has washed their sins away.' "I guess that was supposed to mean something, because he lit up like fireworks on the fourth of July. I tried to act like I understood, but I didn't and he recognized that so he continued. "You see, sister Irene?" Mr. Lands said, "That's what they call everyone, I'm not sure why, but they do." Now she was trying not to laugh as she began to do a little impersonation of the landlord. "Sister Irene, we shout because of the goodness of our God. We worship and praise because our names are written in the book of life."

Oliver interrupted her mid-stride of her version of shouting, "Now listen Irene, I don't think you should be making fun of them. They may be odd but they have been mighty good to you and Robert. It sounds like they went out of their way to take care of you when you moved to Salyersville.

Just because you don't agree with their style of church doesn't mean you should make fun of them." "Daddy, you have no idea." Irene said. However out of respect for her father, she let it go. This scene played out nearly every time Irene and Robert came around. Robert would sit on the couch and Irene would rant and rave over the crazy folks downstairs. When Oliver and Hazel would talk about or refer to Irene, they would always call her 'Sister Irene.' Irene had clearly become consumed by the 'church below' as she called it.

The leaves had fallen to the ground and the days were getting shorter. It was the middle of December and the winds had shifted out of the north. The cold breeze was howling across the valley and occasionally a snowflake would make its way to the ground. Hazel hated winter, but since she was as big as a barrel, she didn't have to worry about getting cold. Nonetheless, she had no plans to be outside unless she just had to. Irene would be there in a little while and the weekend routine would begin.

Robert wasn't going to be coming with her this week because he had to stay home for some weekend work for his company, which meant that Irene would be there all weekend by herself.

"Daddy, are you ready to have Sister Irene here all weekend?" Asked Hazel. "Well yes, Sister Hazel I am." He replied. "You know daddy, that church is really getting to her. I'm starting to worry about her." Hazel said. "Oh she is fine, it gives her something to talk about, maybe a little more than we would like, but at least it's not boring around here. You know, she has that 'shouting thing' down pat?" He said. "Yeah, I don't know if they look as silly as her but if they do, it might be worth the trip to Salyersville." Said Hazel.

"Daddy, have you ever gone to one of those churches? I wonder if they are really as strange as Irene says?" She asked. "I never have been one to go to church and certainly not one of those 'shouting churches." Oliver continued. "Your mom used to go to church, but I figured if her God wasn't able to keep her from dying, he must be a pretty weak God. So after she passed I decided that church was for people who are weak. I do think it's funny to listen to Irene talk about the weird 'church below,' but I have no interest in going to one of their services." Replied Oliver.

Just then it dawned on Hazel that she had never heard about her mom going to church, not that it mattered, but it seems like at some point in her life she would have heard about it. "Daddy, I never knew that momma went to church." Hazel continued. "Was she one of those 'holy rollers' like the people that Irene talks about or was it just casual like Aunt

Martha? Did she take Irene and me to church with her? Did you ever go with her?" "Whoa, whoa, slow down honey that is an awful lot to get to and besides, Irene will be here in just a minute and the last thing I want to be discussing when she gets here is church. You and Sister Irene can have that conversation, but I think I have something better to do right now. That flat needs fixed on the tractor and I have to make sure that the chickens are in so the foxes can't get them." Oliver said.

"Wow daddy, I think it would be easier to talk about church with Irene." Hazel said with a smile. "Yeah, I suppose so, but then Irene would be going home and imitating us." They both laughed as Oliver grabbed his coat and gloves and headed toward the back door. "Daddy," Hazel added, "Can we have that conversation some time? I really would like to know more about mom, even if it was about church." "Sure sweetie, sometime." He answered as he closed the door behind him.

CHAPTER 17

FROM BAD TO WORSE

In the days following the wreck, Matthew laid low. He had tried to find out about the truck driver, but there seemed to be no news. He had decided that no news was good news. After a few more days he figured it was safe enough to take the car and get it fixed so he could make another run. As he walked across the back yard toward the shed Matthew looked anxiously to make sure no one was nearby. Matthew slid the door open and slipped inside to survey the damage, but to his surprise the car was gone. Panic flooded his heart, his mind was racing, "Who had taken the car and what had they done with it?"

The thought of the police having the car was more than he could stand, but if they were the ones to get it he would have heard something by now. He hadn't told anyone about the wreck, not even the people who ran the 'company' as they preferred to be called. He knew enough about them to know they were not to be crossed. If they had the car, all that he could do was set and wait until they brought it back and gave him his next drop. He slipped back out of the shed and toward the house. As he was about to step up on the porch he noticed a truck pull through the alley and slow down. He quickly turned the knob on the door and stepped inside of the house.

Once inside Matthew leaned against the door and peaked out the curtain to see if the truck was still there. He recognized that truck but couldn't remember where he had seen it. He thought to himself, "Who drives an old Chevrolet pickup?" The thought had hardly escaped his mind when he heard a knock at the door. He hadn't noticed the man standing there by the porch and before he knew it, the door was shoved open and he found himself being dragged out onto the back porch.

The feel of the pistol in his rib cage was something he will never forget. There was no chance to defend himself or fight back. He felt a sting in his left side and heard the dull thug. He had never imagined what being shot would feel like, but he knew that he had been. Matthew crumpled to his knees. As he looked up, it dawned on him who this man was and there was no doubt why this was happening to him.

He could feel the warm blood running down his leg, the pain was intensifying but the blow to his right ear took his mind off of the burning sensation in his side. "You will never touch my daughter again!" said the man. "If you ever come near her again, I will finish what I have started." He continued. With that he planted his foot in Matthew's mid section and kicked him over and over until Matthew thought he would die. Mercifully the man took the pistol and slammed the handle into Matthew's temple and knocked him out cold.

When he woke up it was dark outside and Matthew was in more pain than he could imagine. It had begun to rain and he guessed it was the rain that had caused him to come to. He attempted to stand up, but the pain caused him to nearly pass out again. His head was pounding, his body was screaming. He tried again to stand and then wilted back to the ground. He knew he was slipping into unconsciousness, but there was nothing he could do to stop it.

Matthew blinked hard and fought to open his eyes, they burned so bad, he hurt so severely. "Just lay still boy!" He heard a male voice say. "Where am I?" Matthew muttered to the best of his ability. "Don't worry about that right now, you just better be glad we got you when we did or you would be laying in a morgue. You look worse than your car did. Who did this to you? We know it's not from the wreck because there was no blood in the car." Matthew tried hard to answer but his head was spinning and his words were hard to understand. Matthew passed out again.

Some time later Matthew was awakened to a damp cloth being laid across his head. He was able to open one eye and could see an elderly woman staring down at him. "Where am I?" He asked. "You are in your daddy's house." She replied. "Who are you?" asked Matthew. I'm a friend of your dad's." She answered. "He found you laying on the couch, all bandaged up and unconscious. He called me over to make sure that you were okay. What happened to you?" She asked. "I'm not sure, really, I don't remember. Who was the guy that was talking to me?" Matthew asked. "What guy, this is the first time you have woke up. All I know is your dad came in and found you laying here." She answered. Matthew was struggling to make sense of things, but nothing was adding up.

Over the next few weeks he began to regain his strength. Thankfully the bullet had missed his vital organs and other than making a humongous exit wound on his stomach he was relatively okay. His right ear roared all of the time and when someone talked the roaring seemed to intensify.

Matthew realized that he would never hear out of that ear again. He had been so severely beaten that, not being able to hear was the least of his problems. Those kicks to his midsection had caused some major damage. He could hardly walk. He knew he needed to see a doctor, but he also knew better than to go to see one. There was nothing that he could do but sit or lay there.

Matthew had tried to contact the company, but he had no way to reach them. He had been so badly beaten that at times he could hardly complete a sentence without stumbling over words. He was sure that at some point he would get better, but for now there was nothing he could do. His car was gone, his money was gone, and given the way his head roared, he wasn't sure that he could drive if he had a car.

It had been nearly six months since his last run and Matthew was broke. At times he wanted to find the guy that had done this to him, but he knew better, besides there was no way to get to him if he could.

At times Matthew thought he was losing his mind. He was going stir crazy. He had toyed with the idea of going and looking for other work, but his hearing was so bad that he didn't know what kind of work he could do if he could find a job.

One afternoon he heard a knock on the back door. He slowly got up from the sofa and limped toward the door. He looked out through the curtain, there was a sleek black coupe parked in his driveway and Clarence stood there on the porch.

Matthew quickly unlocked the door and opened it for Clarence. Clarence looked at Matthew for a moment before he said anything. "Boy, you are lucky to be alive. When we found you, you were covered in blood and had been lying in the mud for quite a long time. Whoever got ahold of you just about did you in.

Your car was just about as bad as you were, it didn't take long to figure out what happened to it. The newspaper back in Purdin covered the wreck pretty thoroughly. The truck driver is paralyzed from his waste down and the law has looked everywhere for the person that caused the wreck. The driver said he got a pretty good look at you, but his description was vague. " Clarence continued.

"I'm not really sure who did this to you, but as best as we can tell, if they were trying to kill you they nearly got the job done. Don't worry, we took care of the car for you."

"Are you ready to run again?" Clarence asked. "Things have changed at the 'company' and we have expanded our operation." Matthew must have taken a little too much time deciding how to answer so Clarence asked again, "Are you ready to run or not? We have been pretty gracious to you, but we can't wait much longer to figure out whether you are in or out."

"What do you mean 'you have expanded the operation?" Matthew asked. "Well now son, that just really isn't any concern for you. The only thing for you to worry about is whether or not you are in." Matthew was not quick to answer and apparently

Clarence was running thin on patience. "Listen to me boy, you owe us some money and the way I see it, you are either going to work it off or we are going to take it out of you, so you had better figure out real quick which way you want to pay it. Do you understand me?" Matthew knew full well that he had better not get on the bad side of Clarence and whoever the company was because he had already seen how that plays out. He wasn't sure however, how he owed them anything?

He had nearly gotten himself killed working for them and this was their way of showing gratitude? Before he   could catch himself he blurted out, "What do you mean I owe you? I nearly got killed on my last..." Before he could finish, he found himself pinned against the wall with Clarence's hand tight around his throat. "I'm going to tell you one time and you better listen real good, we got rid of your car for you and kept you from going to jail or worse. If you ever raise your voice or question me again, it will be your last time. Now, do you want to work or not? If you do, a car will be waiting for you in the parking lot behind Turner's store. The directions will be in the usual place. If you don't, well let's just say that the boys will be back to see you. I suggest that you be at Turner's by 3:00 pm."

With that Clarence released Matthews throat and turned toward the door. As he turned the knob he looked back over his shoulder at Matthew and said, "We would like to keep you around son, but we can find other drivers." Matthew started to say something, then thought better of it.

Clarence walked out of the house and Matthew still in a daze from being choked glanced at the clock and realized he only had a couple of hours to get cleaned up and ready to go if he was going to make it to Turner's on time. Not being there by 3:00 was not an option. If he didn't show, he was a dead man.

The demands were greater and the stress that had been placed on him was about more than he could bear. The runs they sent Matthew on were further and further away and the stuff he was hauling was now more than shine, he didn't know exactly what the shipments were, but he knew that he was dealing with a different level of people. They were very secretive and saw to it that he knew only where to go and when to get there.

Matthew didn't even care what the supplies were that he was hauling he just saw to it that he got it where it needed to be and on time. There was no doubt that Clarence was no one to be toyed with. He had done hard time and had walked away from a work assignment with a Mississippi chain gang and made it very clear that he would never go back. Matthew was in no mood to find out if he was as mean as some had suggested. As long as they kept the money coming he was more than willing to play it cool and not say anything that would roil anyone up.

CHAPTER 18

A COLD NIGHT IN DECEMBER

A few minutes later Hazel saw the headlights of Irene's car as she turned in to the drive. While it was fun talking 'about' her sister, talking 'to' her was not so much fun. They were like oil and water and since that conversation back in April, well, Hazel dreaded the thought of being stuck in a room with her for any length of time. It was one thing when Robert was there because she knew things wouldn't get too deep. Come to think of it, this was going to be one of the only times since they were kids that she would have to worry about it.

As quickly as she could, Hazel pulled herself up out of the chair and moved toward the back door hoping to make it out before Irene got inside of the house. Hazel reached for her jacket and was nearly to the back door when Irene opened the front door, "Where are you going?" Asked Irene. "Oh, I'll be back in a minute, I'm going out to collect the eggs." Hazel replied. "Where is daddy?" Irene asked. "He is out fixing the flat on the tractor." Hazel answered. "At this time of the evening?" Asked Irene. "It's awful cold out there, why did he decide to work on it after the sun went down and besides how is going to see to do anything out in that old barn?" "Well, I guess he is using a lantern and I don't know why he decided to work on it right now." Hazel answered, although clearly not telling the truth because she knew full well why he decided to do it now. "Anyway, I'll be right back." "Hey wait for me, I want to go tell daddy hi anyway." Irene said.

With that, they headed out the back door. Hazel was moving much slower than her older sister and navigating down the back steps was a little tricky. She waddled to the edge of the steps and grabbed the handrail to begin her decent when she heard Irene scream. "Daddy!" Irene took off at a full sprint toward the barn. As Hazel looked up she saw Oliver lying on the ground by the tractor. "Daddy, are you okay?" Irene continued. Before Hazel could get off of the porch Irene had already reached the front of the garage.

At first she thought that the tractor had somehow fallen on him because of the way he was laying but the closer she got she soon realized that he had collapsed while changing the tire. Irene turned to Hazel and shouted, quick go get help something has happened to daddy. Hazel rushed as fast as possible to the truck and along the way yelled back to her sister, "I'm going down to the Gavin's place, he was a medic in the army, he will know what to do." Irene replied, "I don't care what you do just get help and do it fast."

Hazel climbed in to the truck and drove as fast as she could down the lane to Walter and Louise Gavin's house. Thankfully Mr. Gavin was just getting home and was still in his car. "Quick, Mr. Gavin, we need your help! Something has happened to daddy, he is laying in the yard. Irene is with him but we got to have help!" "Get going girl, I'll follow you." He replied. She couldn't have been gone more than five minutes, but it seemed to take forever.

She was crying uncontrollably and praying, "Please God, spare daddy, I can't bear to lose him. You gotta help him God." The thought occurred to her how silly it was to invoke the help of God when she had never talked to him in the past. She shrugged that thought off and fought back the tears as she pulled in to the drive and down to the barn where her dad was laying. Irene had wetted a towel and was trying to wipe his face to get him to wake up but it hadn't worked. Before Hazel could get out of the car, Henry Gavin was already to her father. "Can you hear me Oliver?" He shouted. He felt his neck to be sure there was a pulse and nodded an affirmative to the girls who were standing over their dad. "Listen, your daddy is alive, but we're going to have to get him over to Dr. Barton's quick. "What's wrong with him Mr. Gavin?" Asked Irene. "I can't be sure, but I think it is his heart." He answered. "Now quick, one of you go get my car and pull it down here fast. Can either of you drive a standard?" He asked. "Yeah we both can." Said Irene as she headed off to the car, not wanting to wait for Hazel to make the trip. She pulled the car as close as possible to her dad and heard Mr. Gavin tell her, "I'm going to need your help, we are going to have to get him in the back seat and your sister here doesn't need to be lifting on him."

As they loaded Oliver in to the car, Mr. Gavin climbed in the back with him and Hazel and Irene got in the front and sped out the drive and up the lane as fast as they could. Mr. Gavin was trying his best to get some kind of response from Oliver, but to no avail. In the back seat they could hear Mr. Gavin working with their dad and they heard him praying out loud for Oliver, "Father God, in the name of Jesus, I need you to help me here. This man's got to live and I'm asking you for a miracle."

Irene thought to pray as well, but she was too embarrassed at the notion after all of the fun she had while laughing and making fun of the 'holy rollers.' She thought it best just to try to concentrate on the road and get her daddy to the hospital. Irene drove as quickly as she could, there was no one on the road and she was glad, tears were blurring her vision and even if her eyes were clear, Hwy 17 was not the straightest road in Eastern Kentucky.

Hazel asked, "Is he breathing Mr. Gavin?" "Yes, he is breathing but his pulse isn't strong and neither are his breaths." He answered. Mr. Gavin continued praying and the faster Irene drove the louder Mr. Gavin prayed. Hazel wondered if it was because he was a little scared of her sister's driving or if her daddy was in that bad of a shape.

"In the name of Jesus!" Henry practically yelled. At once Oliver's body jerked hard and Mr. Gavin could feel him take a deep breath. In a few moments, his pulse seemed to be normal again and his breathing became more regular. "Oliver! Oliver, can you hear me?" Asked Mr. Gavin. Oliver this is Henry, it's Henry Gavin, can you hear me?" "Why yes, yes I can hear you." Oliver whispered.

"Where am I? Where are we going?" He said. "You are in the back seat of my car and we are headed to the hospital to get you checked out. You gave us all a pretty good scare." Henry said. "That was the strangest thing." Oliver said, as his sentence just seemed to trail off. "Don't try to talk Oliver, just rest until we get you to the clinic." Oliver was now breathing regularly; he was soaked with sweat and shivering at the same time. "Are you cold?" Asked Henry. "Yes I am." He answered. Henry took his coat off and laid it across Oliver. "Daddy, I love you!" said Hazel. "I do too daddy." Irene added. "Irene, is that you?" Oliver asked. "Yes daddy, it's me." She said.

Oliver tried to say something more, but Henry told him to lay still and rest. As Irene pulled up to the clinic, Mr. Gavin got out and rushed to the door to find an orderly or someone who could help him get Oliver inside. Hazel opened the door and was just getting out when the orderly came rushing to her side. "Ma'am, you just sit right here in this chair and I will get you inside." He exclaimed.

"Are you in labor?" He asked without waiting for an answer. Hazel was trying to explain that she was not in labor and that it was her daddy in the back seat that needed to be cared for, but he wasn't listening to her. "Oh dear Lord, my first day at the clinic and I got to help deliver a baby! I don't know the first thing about delivering babies." He muttered, clearly exasperated. "Hey!" Irene yelled. "She is not having a baby! We need help with my dad, he's in the back seat!"

By the time the orderly gave up on getting Hazel in the wheel chair, Oliver was already trying to get out of the car on his own. "Wait just a minute Oliver!" Said Mr. Gavin. "You just sit right back down and wait, he's gone through the trouble of getting a wheel chair for you and you are going to use it. I don't know what happened there, but you were in pretty bad shape a few minutes ago, the least you can do is let them check you out."

"Here sir," yelled the orderly, "let's get you in this seat." Oliver did his best to yell back to the orderly but was too weak to do it; still he was able to get his point across. "Why are you yelling?" he asked with as loud of a voice as he could possibly muster. "I'm sick, not deaf!" With a quick apology from the orderly, they rushed Oliver inside. He tried to convince everyone that this was a huge waste of time and that he would be just as well off at home, but Irene and Hazel would have none of it.

"Daddy," cried Irene, "You scared us to death and you have to let them find out what happened." With that the doctor stepped through the door and over to the gurney where Oliver was laying. "Well hello there Ollie. What happened to you?" "James Barton is that you?" asked Oliver. "I haven't seen you since school. How have you been?" "It has been a while hasn't it?" replied Dr. Barton. "Before we rehash the past few years, let's find out what is going on with you, I'm pretty sure these good folks didn't bring you here for a visit."

"No, I suppose they didn't," answered Oliver. Before the girls could ask the question, Dr. Barton gave them answer. "Me and Ollie went to school together and actually dated the same girl, didn't we Ollie?" "As a matter of fact we did, but I was the one who won her, wasn't I?" responded Oliver. "James, these are my daughters, this is Irene and Hazel." The doctor shook their hands and said, "It is a pleasure to meet you both, now that you mention it, they do look like their momma Ollie, by way, where is she?" he asked and immediately caught himself, "Oh I'm sorry, I remember my sister Dotty telling me that she had passed, but I was overseas and couldn't get back for the funeral." I'm sure sorry Ollie, well anyway, it is good to meet you girls." With that he grabbed the gurney and rolled Oliver into an exam room.

A few minutes later Dr. Barton came out of the exam room and sat down at a chair across from Irene, Hazel and Mr. Gavin. "Folks" he said, "I have checked him over as best as I possibly can and quite honestly can't seem to find a problem. I asked him to tell me what happened and he didn't remember anything other than waking up in the back seat of the car talking to Henry Gavin. Can any of you tell me what happened?" Mr. Gavin introduced himself and gave him a run down on Oliver's condition when he got to him. "Are you a doctor sir?" Asked the doctor. "No, no, I was a medic during the war," said Mr. Gavin. "Oh, I see," continued the doctor, "how about you girls, is there anything that you can add that may help? Has he complained about any pains or been short of breath?" Irene looked at Hazel and said, "I live over in Salyersville now and only get home on weekends and I have never heard him complain about anything, Have you Hazel?"

"No, honestly daddy never complains about anything let alone his health," answered Hazel. "He had just walked out the back door not 13 minutes before Irene found him and when he left he seemed to be feeling fine."

"I suppose we should keep him over for tonight and keep an eye on him, that is of course, if we can convince him to stick around. The Oliver Trommel that I remember was somewhat hard headed," Dr. Barton said with a smile. "Thank you for your input Mr. Gavin and for helping an old friend out in his time of need. Ollie and me go back a long way. Girls, I sure hope I didn't upset you when I asked about your momma. She was a good person and her and your dad made a pretty good couple, as bad as it pains me to admit it," he said as he stood up. "If I can convince him to stay, I'll call you back to see him for a minute, if not, he is going to need a ride home, so stick around for a bit if you would Mr. Gavin."

A few minutes later the door opened and instead of the doctor, it was Oliver coming out. "Now daddy, what are you doing? You should be in there laying down." Quipped Irene. "Dr. Barton said you should stay overnight and let him check you over..." The doctor interrupted Irene, "I told you he was hard headed." He would have none of it and insisted that he was fine and would be better sleeping in his own bed and in the company of you girls rather than that old slab that we had him on and having to spend time with the likes of me." "Now James, that is not exactly what I said," replied Oliver. "I just don't think that there is any reason to stay here and let you all prod around looking for something that isn't there. Besides that, James, you might do something to me to get even with me for taking Anna away from you." Oliver said with a half-cocked grin. You could tell that he and the doctor had been good friends and that there were no hard feelings between them. They talked for a few more minutes and after exchanging pleasantries, Henry, Oliver, and the girls made their way to the car.

Other than being a little tired, which considering it was nearly 11:00 pm; Oliver seemed to be back to his old self. "Henry, I'm sorry for all of the trouble I caused you," said Oliver, "I knelt down there by the tractor and was getting ready to fix that tire and the next thing I know, I heard you or someone praying for me and I woke up here in the car."

"It wasn't a problem Oliver, but have you ever had

anything like that happen before?" Asked Mr. Gavin. "No, no I haven't. I don't remember any pains or nothing of the sorts, everything just went black," replied Oliver. "Well daddy, you nearly scared us to death." Said Hazel. "I'm sorry about that girls, you should have just left me to be, I'd been fine," he answered. Henry explained that, to the best of his knowledge, if they had not found him when they did, he might not be alive. "You didn't have much of a pulse when we got you in the car and although I don't know exactly what happened, I can't help but believe that God was giving you another chance." Oliver started to reply, but realized they were just pulling into the drive at his house. "Henry, you are a good neighbor. Would you please tell Louise how sorry I am for keeping you out all night," said Oliver.

CHAPTER 19

AN INVITATION HE COULDN'T REFUSE

Robert had gotten home from work a little later than normal and was just settling in to the comfort of his chair to finalize some paper work when he heard a knock on the apartment door. He laid his papers on the table beside his chair and walked to the door. "Who is it?" He asked. "It's Walter Lands, can I bother you for a minute?" "Certainly you can and it's no bother." Robert replied as he opened the door and stretched out his hand to Mr. Lands. "Come in, come in." said Robert. "Why thank you Robert, I won't take but a minute of your time, I just wanted to let you know that we are having a special service tonight and would like to invite you." Before Robert could reply, Mr. Lands continued, "You remember that family that lost their son in that house fire don't you? Well of course you do, that's why you all stayed here isn't it? Anyway..." Walter continued, not waiting for Robert to answer him. "Reverend Nelson, you remember him don't you? Well, he led that family to the Lord a couple of months back and the good Lord has called Brother Williams to preach the Gospel and tonight is going to be his first time preaching."

While Walter paused to catch his breath, Robert quickly interjected, "I appreciate you asking Walter, but I am really behind on some paper work and need to get it done. Irene went home to her dad's and I stayed here in hopes of catching up." "Well now son, if you change your mind, we would sure love to have you join us." Answered Mr. Lands. "We are going to have some refreshments later on, so maybe you could at least join us after service." "If I get done, I just might do that." Answered Robert.

As Robert settled back into his chair and began his work, he could hear the old door slam open and hit the wall. "Why doesn't someone fix that thing?" He said aloud. Again and again the door opened, the best he could tell, there must me a thousand people down stairs by now. He knew there probably wasn't more than the usual 30 to 73 but it sounded like there were many more. He looked up at the clock hanging over the kitchen door and started counting down. "Ten, nine, eight, seven, six, five, four, three, two and..." "Well good evening everyone!" Said Reverend Nelson. Robert had it down pat. "I'll say one thing for the good reverend, he always starts on time." Robert said to himself.

It was hard to focus on his work with all of the singing going on down stairs. On some songs he could hear the men bellowing out the words to songs that now had become quite familiar to him. Then he heard one of the most beautiful voices that he could recall, she was singing soft but it seemed to be carrying into his apartment as though the door was wide open. He laid his papers aside and sat there listening, the words seem to reach into his soul and it was as though he could hear nothing else:

"Oh, love of God, how rich and pure!

How measureless and strong!

It shall forevermore endure-

The saints and angels' song."

Before he knew what was happening and before he could ever stop it, not that he wanted to anyway, Robert felt a hot tear form in his eye and drop off of his cheek. That one tear was followed by what felt like a river. 'What in the world has come over me,' He thought. He wiped his eyes but there was no stopping the flow, without as much as a second thought, Robert walked over to the door and stepped into the stairwell that led down to the place where it seemed that angels were gathered. By the time that he had made it to the bottom step, he was sobbing uncontrollably. Robert never waited for anyone to give the invitation; he just walked straight down the center aisle of the makeshift church and collapsed in a sobbing ball at the altar. The place went crazy.

There must have been 30 or 40 men praying for him or with him and it was like heaven had just enveloped him. It felt like a million pounds had been lifted from his shoulders and somehow Robert knew what being saved really meant. He also knew why these folks act like they do. With tears cascading down his face, Robert looked over at one of the men and said, "I want everything God has for me!" Again the place erupted. There were people leaping and jumping, one of the fellows just took off running around the place. Robert let out what sounded like a war hoop!

He didn't know how long he had been there in the floor but it didn't matter. It didn't even matter that he hadn't got his work done. What he had just experienced was so much more than he could wrap his brain around. People were singing and shouting and clapping and dancing and without another thought Robert found himself hugging people he didn't know and shouting right along with them. Brother Williams never did get to preach that night, but no one seemed too upset about that. Finally after a few hours, although it seemed like only a few minutes, Reverend Nelson took the stage. "Well Brother's and Sister's, there is shouting going on in Heaven and on earth tonight!" He said. "Praise God for Robert's salvation, can I get an amen?"

Reverend Nelson asked Brother Williams if he would preach for them on Sunday night since there "sure won't be any preaching tonight!" He added. Brother Williams assured him that he would be honored to and after a few announcements the service was dismissed and everyone gathered for refreshments. Robert was still overwhelmed by the tremendous sense of peace that had swept not only over him but also through him. They tried to get him to stay and fellowship, but he had no interest in food, he just wanted to soak in this feeling as long as he could. Instead of climbing the 19 steps that led to the upstairs apartment, Robert felt like he was floating.

Once inside the apartment Robert returned to the chair where he had been sitting earlier that evening. His mind drifted off to thoughts of Irene. "I wonder what Irene will think about me being one of those shouters?" He said, almost breaking into laughter. As he sat there he began to talk to God about his life and how grateful he was that things had worked out the way they had for he and Irene. Not that he was thankful that someone's house burned to the ground or that they lost their child, no, that was horrible. Yet somehow through all of that tragedy, God had guided he and Irene to an upstairs apartment with nothing to block the sound of the church services down below. Those thin walls that were often a cause for cursing, were now the greatest blessing that he had ever known.

Robert began to thank God once again for all of the events that had led him to his new found faith and then he began to pray for Irene. He surmised that she would be somewhat amused by his decision and probably would question his sanity. She may even be upset at him for being so foolish as to let his emotions get the best of him. Is that what it was? He thought. Was it just my emotions getting the best of me? No, he knew better. Something had happened that no one would ever be able to talk him out of and he would never be able to dismiss as just an emotional reaction.

The peace that had swept over him that night was so incredible. Again he found himself in awe at this God who loved him so much that he positioned him at this place and in this moment to show him his love. Praise and adoration began to flow from his heart and out of his mouth. Once again, the same power and presence that had enveloped him earlier swept over and through him. It was as though God himself had walked into his apartment and shut all of heaven down just to spend time with Robert Trommel.

As he contemplated all that had taken place that evening the one thing that seemed so amazing was how free he felt. Until now he had never considered himself to be bound or for that matter a sinner. Now it was as though the weight of the world had been rolled from his heart and he knew that he would never be the same. He also noticed the stack of unfinished paper work that was scattered on the side table by where he had been sitting a few hours earlier. He had wondered what would have happened if Irene was home at the time. Would she have responded the same way? While Robert wasn't sure how Irene would react to his decision to become a Christ follower or as she would probably say, a 'holy roller,' he knew the incredible peace that now filled his heart was the best thing that ever happened to him.

He needed some sleep, but as he looked over to his side table, Robert reached the conclusion that the work he had put off earlier in the evening wasn't going to get done by itself. He went into the kitchen to get a glass of water, and had barely made it back to

MOMENTS-THE STORY OF GIL AND MACEY

his chair when he was overtaken with a sudden urging to begin praying for Oliver. He sat in his chair trying to make sense of what it was that he was feeling, he thought maybe it would go away, but instead of it fading, he felt it getting stronger and stronger. It seemed almost like an audible voice telling him to pray for Oliver.

Robert fell to his knees and gripped the side of the chair where he had been sitting. "Oh God, I don't know what is going on, but I am asking you to please touch Oliver. Please be with him! If there is something wrong with him I am asking you to please keep him in your care. He wasn't sure if he was praying correctly or not, he hadn't really had an opportunity to learn how to pray, but somehow he could feel his prayers working.

More important than his prayers working, he had a growing confidence that God was at work and whatever it was that had happened or was wrong with his father in law, was now being turned around. He wasn't sure how long he had prayed, but he knew of a certainty that God had heard his prayers. After what seemed like only a few minutes Robert felt a release, he felt the burden lift. In truth it had been much longer. When he looked at the clock to see the time he realized that he had been praying for nearly an hour.

He couldn't wait for Irene to get home so that he could tell her what had happened and to see if she knew anything that may have been wrong with her dad. Again Robert found himself meditating on how good God was. The more he praised God the more he felt God. It was like a gentle river flowing over and through him.

Somewhere during this heavenly visitation he had fallen into the deepest sleep of his life. "It's amazing how well you can sleep when your heart is at rest." Reverend Nelson would later tell him. It was true he knew that his heart was at rest. The next thing he heard was the sound of the 2000-pound door of the furniture store slamming against the wall down stairs. Robert rolled over and to his surprise it was daylight. Not only daylight, but if the furniture store was open for business it must be at least nine. "Holy Smokes!" Shouted Robert. "I have slept the day away." Then he remembered the stack of papers that were awaiting his attention. He bolted out of bed more rested than he could ever remember.

By noon he had finished all of his work and straightened up the apartment. As Robert sat down in his chair to relax, he felt the sudden urge to read the Bible. "I wonder where Irene put that Bible we got as a wedding present?" He said. Her cousin Helen had given them a family Bible when they got married. It was so large that they often discussed using it as an end table, so he knew she couldn't have carried it too far. Then he remembered the box of keepsake items that he had put up in the top of the coat closet. How could he have forgotten that box, he griped the entire time he was putting it up there because it was so heavy. He had been standing on an old half broken chair and Irene was holding it with all the strength that she could muster so that it didn't snap in pieces under Robert.

He looked around the apartment for something to stand on that would be more secure than that old chair. He knew better than to get one of the new ones that they had bought from the furniture store. If he broke one of them, he would never hear the end of it. He surmised. With that he grabbed the rickety chair from the corner and carried it over to the closet door. "Help me Lord!" Robert prayed out loud. He wedged the back of the chair against the edge of the door frame and reached as high as he could and pulled the old box full of keepsakes down on his shoulder.

To his surprise the chair didn't break but the box did. Papers were strewn across the floor and the Bible that he had been looking for found him. It landed on the edge of his right foot and since he hadn't taken time to put his shoes on yet, he felt the weight of it on his big toe. He must have yelled pretty loud because at once the door to the apartment burst open and in came Mr. Lands. "What in the world? Are you alright son?" Shouted Walter Lands. "I heard that bang and you scream and thought I had better check on you. Forgive me for bursting in like that, I just didn't know..." Said Walter. His voice trailed off as he saw the papers scattered across the floor and Robert holding is right foot.

"Oh, I'm alright." Said Robert. "Thanks for checking on me though, I never thought about the noise that it must have made downstairs, please forgive me if I scared anyone." He added. "Is there something that I can help you with while I'm up here?" Asked Mr. Lands. "No, no. The only thing that I hurt was my foot and my pride." Robert replied with a laugh. "Well, okie-doke, but if you need me, don't hesitate to ask." Mr. Lands said. "Well, there is one thing that you could help me with if you don't mind." Robert continued, "I'm trying to figure out how to tell Irene what happened last night and I'm not sure the best way to do it. I honestly don't know how she will respond. If I just say, 'Hey Irene, while you were home this weekend, I became a Holy Roller!' No disrespect intended, but she will probably have to pick herself up off of the floor.

"I take that she doesn't have a flattering opinion of us 'holy rollers?' Asked Walter. "Oh she has a very high opinion of you, um of us, well, what I'm trying to say is..." Robert stammered looking for the right way to say what he was trying to say.

Mr. Lands came to his rescue. "Let me tell you my story Robert, maybe that will help. You see, I was serving in the army and was about to be discharged when I got the letter from Margaret telling me..." Mr. Lands was mid sentence when Robert cut him off. "Pardon the interruption, but who is Margaret?" Asked Robert as he bent down to gather up the papers. "That's my wife's name, didn't I introduce you by name when you all came to look at the apartment?" He asked. "Oh no sir, I don't think so, but please continue, I'm sorry for cutting you off." He answered. "Well I was getting ready to be discharged and I got the letter from Margaret, my wife. She told me that the previous week she had gone to a brush harbor meeting with her friend Emma and..." Again Robert interrupted. "I'm really sorry, but what is a brush harbor meeting?" He said. "That is exactly what I asked Margaret in my reply letter, but anyway, she said that at this brush harbor meeting she had given her life to Christ and was baptized in the Holy Ghost.

Before you ask, I didn't know either." Continued Mr. Lands with a chuckle. "Anyway, Margaret went on to tell me how her new found salvation made her feel and how she couldn't wait for me to get home so I could go with her to the church that had started as a result of the brush harbor." He continued. "My mind was racing as I was trying to understand what all of this 'brush harbor, Holy Ghost' stuff had to do with me and why she thought I needed religion. I sent her a letter asking her the questions that you are wanting to ask me right now, but I got released and was home before I received her reply."

By this time Robert had gathered up the keepsake papers and the Bible and had asked Mr. Lands to join him in the living room for the continuation of the story. Mr. Lands never skipped a beat; his eyes were wide and full of excitement as he continued. "I got home not really knowing what to expect, honestly I thought she had gone off of the deep end and would be burning candles and setting around mumbling some kind of something. Well, to be truthful, I didn't know what I would find." "What did you find? Asked Robert. "I'm getting there son." He answered. "I got off of the bus and there she stood. More beautiful than ever, she had the biggest smile that you could imagine. She, well, she looked normal. As we walked home from the bus station, all that seemed different was how happy she was. I thought maybe it was because I was home and was safe, but it was more than that. There was a joy about her that I couldn't describe. She didn't preach me a sermon or tell me that I needed to get religion, she just let me see what a wonderful change her Lord had made in her."

"I see what you are saying Mr. Lands." Said Robert. "Please son, call me Walter." He said. "Yes sir, I will. You are saying that all I really need to do is just live the change that took place and God will take care of the rest?" Asked Robert. "Yes, I guess that is what I'm saying in so many words." Answered Walter. "By the way, how long is Irene going to be gone, it snowed pretty good last night and they are calling for more today. You don't think she will try driving home in this weather do you?" He asked.

"I didn't know that we got any snow? Said Robert. "I guess I hadn't thought to look outside, Robert continued. I don't know, but if it's bad surely she won't try driving in the snow. She isn't very confident in her driving abilities on clear roads, she would be terrified to drive ..." Roberts words trailed off as he made his way to the window. It looked like there were at least six or seven inches of snow on the street below. "Are you alright, son?" Asked Mr. Lands. "I'm fine, but I am really worried that Irene will try to drive home and I know how scared she must be. I just wish there was a way that I could get a message to her to stay put until this storm is over." Mr. Lands stopped Robert mid sentence and said, "Listen son, we may not be able to get a message to her, but we can sure get one to our heavenly Father. He knows just what we need before we pray and he also knows where Irene is and what she needs. Let's go to the Lord in prayer."

Robert and Walter knelt there by the window and began praying for Irene and asking God to either speak to her and tell her to stay put at her dad's or if she had begun the trip back to Salyersville, that he would somehow keep her safe. They had prayed for about 30 minutes when Walter, stood to his feet. "Son, I feel like she is going to be okay." Robert looked up at Mr. Lands.

He could tell that Walter believed what he had said, but either because of fear or concern, he wasn't ready to quit praying. "Walter, thank you for praying with me. I wish that I had the peace that you have, but I feel like I should continue to pray." Said Robert. "You go ahead son, I'm going to get back downstairs and see if Margaret needs some help, but I will keep praying." Mr. Lands said, as he turned to leave. When he got to the door, he looked back over toward Robert and again assured him that everything was going to be fine. Do you recon she'll be back by Sunday?" He asked. "I think she will be back Sunday afternoon around three." Replied Robert. "Remember Brother Nelson is going to be preaching Sunday night, maybe she will come with you to hear him?" Walter said. "I'll sure ask her to and between now and then, you and I can pray that she will." Robert answered.

"Walter, thank you for checking on me and thank you for telling me a little bit of your story, sometime maybe you can tell me the rest of it." Walter walked back over to Robert and wrapped his arms around him and said, "Welcome to the family of God son!" Then he walked back to the door and headed back down stairs.

CHAPTER 20

ANOTHER CHANCE

Oliver and the girls waved goodbye to Mr. Gavin and went into the house. Oliver seemed to be a little troubled and told the girls, "If you don't mind, I'm going to wash up and get some rest girls. It's been a long day." They all said good night and each of them headed off to bed. "Daddy," said Irene, "if you need anything through the night, please wake us up. I don't know what we would do if something happened to you." "Now, now, nothing is going to happen to me, so don't you worry," he answered. "Let's get some rest and we will have time to talk tomorrow. I think I'm going to hang around the house most of the day tomorrow, that is of course, after I fix that tractor tire." "Oh no you're not, you are going to let that go for another day!" Exclaimed Hazel. "Good night girls, I love you and I'm glad you are both here tonight" he said.

They each went to bed and both Hazel and Irene went to sleep fairly quickly but Oliver just lay there. His body was tired but his mind was racing. He was trying to piece together all of the events and make sense of everything that had happened to him but there was just too much to process. He hadn't been entirely truthful with his old friend Dr. Barton or with the girls.

As Oliver lay there looking up at the ceiling his eyes

began to well up with tears. He hadn't cried in a very long time, actually, the last time he cried was when Anna passed away. Was it James Barton's mention of her that had his mind whirling? No, it was more than that, much more than that.

He rehearsed the previous evening over in his mind a thousand times, the conversation with Hazel about her momma going to church, he remembered grabbing his coat and going out to work on the tractor, he could even recall kneeling down there beside it and starting to loosen the eight lug nuts but why couldn't he recollect what happened that sent him to the hospital. He had been thinking about Anna as he walked out to the tractor, that much he knew. Specifically, he could remember thinking of all that had happened since that March night 13 years earlier when she had passed. Oliver thought about how excited she would be to know that she was going to be a grandma.

Why would the God that she loved so much, not heal her. He had thought about how unfair it was for God to leave him with two little girls who desperately needed a momma. As he walked toward the barn, he couldn't help but replay all of the many events that followed her passing. What bothered him most, both before the event the previous evening and now laying there watching the room in the moonlight, was how lonely he had felt and honestly still felt. He glanced over to the right of his bed and his eyes fastened on the picture that still hung there.

Anna was only 21 years old when she had it painted for him and gave it to him as a Christmas present. That was just before she found out that she was...his thought trailed away. "I can't do this!" he thought aloud. "I can't let my mind go there."

It was too late, Oliver's mind was already there and it hurt as bad now as it did watching her decline. Hazel was barely a year old and needed her so desperately but Anna was failing so quickly. She had lost weight so fast and was too weak to even hold her girls let alone take care of them. Those few months went by so quickly that he never felt like he got to say goodbye. Every minute of the day was spent trying to tend to her as she became weaker and frailer. When Anna was sleeping or at least resting he tried to keep the girls occupied or out of the way as much as possible. Then before he knew what hit him, he walked in one morning after gathering eggs, to find that Anna had passed in her sleep.

They say time heals all wounds but these wounds were as deep now as they had ever been. Truth be told, he had wished that he had been the one to die. He knew of course that, although it would have been easier for him, Anna's life would have been anything but easy. Still he lay there struggling with all of the emotions that he had long since put to bed. Oliver drifted off for just a moment, but then suddenly snapped back to consciousness as he recalled something else. The only other thing that bothered him was how angry he was at Anna's God, and... at

Matthew Thompson.

Now as he lay there thinking, he found himself
fighting the same feelings of rage that had led him to
do something, which, although he was ashamed of, it
was so uncharacteristic for him. Certainly Matthew
had it coming to him and there was no doubt that he
hadn't been the first person who had attempted to
kill him. Just then it dawned on him how close he
had come to killing a man, at first he thought he had
succeeded but was relieved to find out that Matthew
didn't die. His mind began to replay the drive to Inez
that nearly ended in a bad way. It wasn't that
Matthew didn't deserve it, oh no, he deserved every
ounce of punishment he got and then some.

Oliver had been able to justify his attempted murder.
He deserved it after all of the pain he had put Hazel
through. It was also for the pain that was facing the
baby Hazel was carrying. Still the thought of that
June morning played over and over in his mind.

The drive to Inez was otherwise uneventful, there
was very little traffic on the road, the air that flowed
through the wing glass on the driver's side window of
his pickup was cool and the smell of early summer
was enough to help settle the nerves. The closer he
got to Inez the more nervous he became. He had
done his homework and knew where Matthews house
was, the only problem was he didn't have any idea
whether or not he would actually catch him home.
How would it all play out? Oliver thought at one
point that the best thing to do would be to turn

around and just let it go.

No sooner had the thought passed through his mind that he remembered the look on Matthew's face the night when Hazel got out of the car. The spineless coward never even had the decency to speak to her or for that matter to him. He remembered Matthews smirk, he remembered the countless times he had watched his baby cry. He thought of all of those mornings that we would lay in bed too sick to get up. This emboldened him all the more. "He has this coming to him," Oliver said aloud. As he turned down the back alley off of Rainier Street, he watched as Matthew slipped from the shed and hurried quickly toward the house.

Oliver killed the engine and engaged the clutch. The truck slowly coasted to a stop behind the shed at the edge of the alley. He didn't know if he had been seen but at this point, didn't care. He wasn't sure how things were going to play out. He had driven to Inez a number of times trying to work up the nerve to take care of Matthew Thompson, but this time he had made up his mind, this was not going to be a dry run. He slipped out of the truck and looked around. Thick trees lined the alley and there was no sign of anyone in any direction.

After tucking the pistol into his waste band, he did his best to cover it with his shirt. He moved to the edge of the shed and as quickly as he could move, ran to the corner of the house by the back porch, took a deep breath and knocked on the door. He was standing to the edge of the porch and out of view when he saw the door handle turn and the door open. The next few moments were hazy, but he could hear the sound of the deep thud of the P38 Walther pistol as he fired the shot into Matthews right side. Matthew crumpled to the ground, as he was going down, Oliver took the butt of the pistol and slammed it into his ear. As he lay there on the porch, Oliver began to stomp him as hard as he possibly could. At first he had a sense of the thrill of having fixed Hazels problem once and for all, but then as he watched Matthew fall off of the edge of the porch and onto the ground, fear swept over him.

What had he done and what if he got caught? Who would take care of Hazel? He turned and ran as fast as he could to the truck, he climbed in and slid behind the wheel and as he reached for the ignition he bumped the horn with his left hand. Oliver fumbled with the keys. He tried desperately to put the key in the ignition, but is seemed to take forever. Finally he was able to put the key in the ignition, but trying to turn it was difficult, his hands were shaking uncontrollably. Had he drawn attention to himself? Had someone heard the slight honk of the horn? Finally after what seemed an eternity he started the truck pressed on the gas and released the clutch. The truck bolted a little faster than he had intended. Oliver sped down the gravel alley and onto Forshee Street.

He looked in his rearview mirror to see if anyone was

behind him and to his delight, saw no one. He took a deep breath and shifted into third gear and as he raised his hand up from the gearshift to the steering wheel he noticed the blood. Oliver knew that it was Matthews blood and not his own, but that didn't serve to calm him any. He had laid the gun in the floorboard by the gearshift and noticed that it too had blood on it. He fumbled in his back pocket trying to find the handkerchief that he always carried. Drawing it out he began to try to wipe the blood from his hand. The reality of what he had done was like flood waters and they seemed to be drowning him.

No matter how hard he wiped, the blood wouldn't come off! Oliver thought for a moment as he came to the edge of Inez and hit highway 19, "I've got to find somewhere to clean up, I've got to get this blood washed off" he was talking aloud and that too scared him. How could he be sure that no one saw him? He had only gone a few miles when he crossed the Shawnee Creek Bridge; just past the bridge he noticed a gavel lane that led down to the edge of Shawnee Creek. Oliver pulled down the lane and quickly washed in the creek, taking special care in cleaning the blood from his gun and gearshift as well as the steering wheel. The rest of the drive home, he would catch himself physically shaking. "For some reason I thought it would make me feel better," he said. "I've got to get ahold of myself. I've got to pull it together."

Over the next few weeks he had done his best to busy himself as far away from town as he could get. He checked the paper regularly and to his surprise, never one word about the shooting in Inez. Oliver was certain that Matthew had recognized him, but perhaps not.

One day while picking up supplies at the lumberyard he ran into Fred Pickens. Fred was a rough neck to say the least; he talked very coarse and was someone that most people would shy away from. They had more in common than either one of them had known. Fred had two daughters and they were about the same age as Oliver's girls and both of the men had a severe hatred for the man who had violated their daughters.

Their girls had gone to school together, at least until Irene got married and quit school. "Oliver!" Yelled Fred, "How in the world are you?" Fred came running from half way across the lumberyard. "Oliver, I ain't seen you for months." "I'm just fine Fred, how about you?" Replied Oliver. "Oh I'm doing pretty well I guess. I suppose you heard about my Helen didn't you?" Asked Fred. "I don't guess so." Answered Oliver, although that wasn't all together true. Irene had told him that someone had taken advantage of Helen, but no one had ever said any more about it. "What happened to her Fred? Is she alright?" Asked Oliver. "Oh yeah, she is fine now, but I don't know how well the punk is that hurt her?" "Me and a couple of the boys caught up with him

MOMENTS-THE STORY OF GIL AND MACEY

down the road past your place a few months ago and worked him over pretty good." Fred said with a smile on his face.

Oliver's heart was pounding so loudly he thought Fred would be able to hear it. "Out past my place?" Asked Oliver. "Yeah, down by highway five." Answered Fred. "Oh yeah, who was the guy?" Oliver asked. "Matthew Thompson is his name and, I don't mind telling you, he ain't worth killing with a club!" Replied Fred. Oliver nearly fell over. "Are you alright Ollie?" Fred asked. "Oh yeah, I'm fine, I just, I just got choked. Anyway, you say Helen is okay huh?" Inquired Oliver. "She'll be alright, but if I ever catch that piece of trash around these parts I'm going to finish him off" Fred continued. "One of my brother in laws is a deputy and he was telling me that someone nearly did it for me, but the Thompson boy lived through it. The law is onto that punk, but they just can't seem to catch him with the goods. They are pretty sure that he is running some shine. I told my buddies to give me a few minutes with him and they won't need to worry about him anymore. I have their assurance that they're going to look the other way, if you know what I mean?" Oliver knew exactly what he meant. He knew Fred well enough to know that he would do exactly what he said. He also knew that if Fred said the law was going to look the other way, that meant that no one would care or notice if Matthew disappeared.

Oliver tried to act oblivious to the depths of Fred's

163

words, but they hit him hard. Did Fred know that it was Oliver that shot Matthew? Thankfully Fred changed the conversation away from Matthew Thompson, but the next subject was not much easier to talk about. "How is your little girl doing Ollie?" continued Fred. "I heard she was in the family way, is that right? Now I don't mean to be nosey, but I heard the girls talking amongst themselves the other night about how sick she has been and when I asked what was wrong, they told me about it." "Oh uh well," Oliver fumbled for words, "She is doing okay I suppose." Truthfully, he had been too occupied with everything else to really know, "she's a strong girl, and she'll be alright."

Fred put his hand on Oliver's shoulder and looked him right in the eyes, "Ollie, who did it to her? If it was Thompson, I'm going to finish what I started. Ollie, I'll kill him." Oliver knew that Fred was serious and as bad as he had wanted to kill Matthew himself, he knew that it wouldn't solve anything, and it wouldn't change the situation at all. "Well Fred, I would rather not talk about that if it's okay with you." Continued Oliver, "Me and Hazel have an awful lot to sort through right now and I don't think we need to add anything else to the mix. Don't get me wrong, I appreciate your willingness to take care of that Thompson boy, but he really isn't worth it." Oliver said. "Well, he'll get his, I promise you that, and Ollie, if you or your little girl need anything you just let me know." Said Fred.

They shook hands and Oliver went inside as Fred continued across the yard. He wandered if Fred knew that he had been the one who nearly killed Matthew Thompson, but surmised, if Fred knew he did it, everyone would know. Thankfully, Fred was too absorbed in his own anger to delve into anyone else's struggles.

As Oliver lay there thinking about Matthew, he breathed a sigh of relief for a couple of reasons, one because he hadn't killed the guy and two because he knew that no one had tied him to the attempted murder. Oliver looked again toward the picture of his dear wife and thought about how much had changed since her passing. Then he remembered something about that trip to the hospital that he hadn't shared with anyone, and as far has he was concerned, never would.

He remembered seeing his body laying there in the backseat with Walter working on it. It was like he was above it all and helpless to respond to anything that was going on. He could hear Walter praying for him and suddenly everything started getting black. He couldn't see Walter, he no longer could see Irene driving, everything was dark, darker, and blacker than one could imagine and the sense of being alone was overwhelming. He could still hear Walter praying for him but it seemed that he was drifting further and further away. It seemed as though it had lasted forever, and then something amazing happened.

Suddenly he felt his body jerk and knew that he was back. What had happened? Was this what death is like? Had he just died? If this was death, where was he going? Now Oliver began to shake. At once he heard himself crying out to a God that he wasn't even sure existed, "Oh God, I don't know why you spared me, I don't understand any of this. Please help me to know what is going on." Oliver couldn't seem to get his mind to rest, but he felt like his body was at a breaking point.

He sat up on the side of the bed and stared out the window across the farm toward the tractor. A light snow had begun to fall and the tractor already had a slight dusting covering it. He thought for a moment that he should go out and cover it over but after the evening that he had, he surmised that it probably wasn't a good idea. After a few minutes of watching the falling snow, Oliver felt his body twitch and realized that he was nodding off sitting there. He lay back on his pillow, looked once again at Anna's picture and then drifted off to sleep.

CHAPTER 21

COMING TO GRIPS

Irene had no idea what kind of war was going on in her daddy's mind, but she was very much aware of her own struggles. Trying to grasp or absorb the events of that Friday night proved much too difficult for her. "What a night!" She thought to herself. It had been an incredible evening and Irene sat down in the chair in the corner of the room and breathed a long sigh of relief. Relieved that the night had come to an end and most of all because her dad was still with them.

There is no way to process the events of the evening or the emotions that had swept over her. From the moment that she walked into the house everything just seemed to escalate. Irene desperately needed to talk, she had been missing her momma something fierce and she also felt like she owed her dad and sister an apology. Robert had been working long hours and it had given Irene a lot of time to think about how she had treated her sister. It wasn't Hazel's fault that their mother had passed away, but Irene realized just how horribly she had treated her. Both of them had missed out on having a mother, but at least she had memories of her momma, Hazel had none. There were no memories of bedtime stories or having her hair brushed, not one single memory of her mother's beautiful smile. Irene had come to realize just how selfish she had been and how heartless she had been toward Hazel.

She had blamed God and become so enraged at Him because he never healed her mom that she took it out on Hazel. The more she thought about it the more guilty she felt. Somehow in her mind she had come to grips with her mom's passing and had even come to some degree of reconciliation with God over the matter. While it didn't make the pain go away it did help her find peace and yet as she had watched her dad nearly slip away that evening she realized just how short life is and how important it is to hold every moment as tight as you possibly can.

She had planned on having this conversation with Hazel and her daddy but now she found herself sitting alone in the bedroom wishing there was someone to talk to. "God," she said. "I don't really know how or what to say to you, but I feel like I need to tell you how grateful I am for you giving daddy back to us tonight." She continued, "I've heard the church people downstairs talking about how good you are and that you will hear even the simplest prayers, so I'm asking you to hear mine." Irene continued. "I don't really understand what happened tonight. Thank you for Mr. Gavin and fixing it so that he would be home and help us get daddy to the hospital. I don't know what we would have done if we would have lost him."

Her prayer faded and her mind raced as she began to relive the past few years. There was such a deep sense of regret for the way that she had treated Hazel and for not spending time with her dad. She thought of Robert and how desperately she wished that he had come with her this weekend. "Of all of the weekends for him not to be with her?" Irene thought. She knew that if there was a way he would have come, he enjoyed getting out of Salyersville as much as her, although neither of them particularly like staying at his folks house. Robert's workload had been pretty intense over the past few weeks and on top of that, she had been riding him pretty hard to find them a house. She was so tired of that apartment, so tired of the noise.

Maybe it wasn't the noise that bothered her as much as an overwhelming sense of guilt, but for what? She wasn't really sure. Was she feeling guilty for making fun of the all of the people and how they worshiped? She had long since decided that the church folk meant well. Although some of them were a little eccentric, for the most part they were really caring people. Irene regularly mocked their services and would even slip out on to the top of the stairs to watch them, she must admit that there were times that she found herself looking forward to the singing that always seemed to find it's way up the stairs and into their apartment. Irene had decided to tell her family how bad she felt about laughing at the church folk.

Then she wondered if they might think that she was turning into one of those 'Holy Rollers.' "There was no way she was going to start acting like those folks." Irene said aloud. Still, she couldn't escape the thoughts of the genuine concern and love they had, not just for each other, but also for everyone.

When the Turner family lost everything, including one of their children in the house fire, the people of the church went above and beyond to take care of them. They had dinners, raised money and brought in clothes. You name it and they did it. "It was genuine too." She thought.

"I don't know how that family can lose a child and not lose their minds." Irene thought as she arose and walked across the room to try to clear her head. She looked out the window and watched the snow as it began to come down. It looked so peaceful. She only wished that her own life were as peaceful as the one that she viewed out the window of the bedroom. The big flakes were already beginning to cover the ground and as Irene watched for a few minutes' two things occurred to her. "If it keeps this up very long, I don't know how I'm going to get home?" She thought. The second thing that occurred to her was that she had never brought her things in from the car.

Irene quickly grabbed her coat and wrapped her scarf around her neck and slipped out of her room and through the living room toward the door. She noticed the light was still on in her dad's room, which given the circumstances, seemed a little strange. Irene stepped toward the door with every intention to knock and make sure that her dad was okay, but thought it would be intrusive. As she turned to go back toward the living room door Hazel startled her.

MOMENTS-THE STORY OF GIL AND MACEY

"What are you doing up?" Asked Irene. "I heard someone walking and decided to make sure that everything was okay. I'm sorry if I scared you Irene." Whispered Hazel. "What are you doing? Are you leaving?" Hazel asked. "No, I forgot to bring my things in when I got here tonight and I was going out to the car to get them." Answered Irene. "Do you need some help?" Asked Hazel, although it was clear that she would be no help. Not only was she nearly nine months pregnant, but also she was dressed for bed.

"No, I can get it, but why are you still awake?" Irene asked. "Shouldn't you be resting?" Irene actually sounded concerned. It caught Hazel off guard to hear the genuine concern in Irene's voice. "Yes, I suppose I should be, but who could rest after the evening that we had." Hazel answered. "Do you think Daddy is going to be alright? Continued Hazel. "I felt so helpless tonight." "Yeah, me too." Exclaimed Irene. "I thought he was going to..." Irene's voice trailed off, as she couldn't make herself finish the sentence. "Don't say it Irene, you don't have to. I feared the same thing. If Mr. Gavin hadn't been home I don't know what may have happened."

Irene stood by the front door for a few moments without moving as she thought about what could have been. She wiped a tear from her cheek and turned the knob and then stepped into the cold night air. The snowflakes seemed to be as big as nickels and the air was so sharp it nearly took her breath.

She looked up toward the sky as the snow fell lightly on her face, Irene whispered a prayer; "Dear God, I don't really know what to say, but I know that it was you that kept daddy from dying tonight. I feel guilty for asking you to do it after all that I have done, but," Just then a cold wind swept across her face and a hard chill shot up her back interrupting her prayer. Irene stepped down off of the porch and slowly walked toward the car. "I wonder what Robert is doing tonight?" She thought to herself.

She wished that he were there with her. Of all of the times when he couldn't come why did it have to be this time? Then again, if he had been with her they would not have gone to get Mr. Gavin and then what would have happened to her dad? That thought was more than she could bear. She could still hear Henry Gavin shout, "In the name of Jesus!" When he yelled that she had practically ran off of the road. There was something so powerful about the way that man prayed. It's not that she hadn't heard people yell; no she had become pretty accustomed to that. They did a lot of praying and shouting and yelling down stairs at the church, but she knew that something had happened in the backseat of that car that night. There was no denying it, and she also knew that whatever had happened, it was because of Jesus.

Irene brushed the freshly fallen snow away from the door handle of the car and opened it. She retrieved her bag of clothes, closed the door and turned toward the house. Her dad's light was still on and for a moment she thought again to check on him, but thought it best to try to get some sleep. She hurried back to the porch and into the house, brushed the snow off of her shoes and quietly returned to her room. Hazel had gone back to her room and Irene was okay with that. Her mind was whirling and conversation was the last thing on her wish list.

Irene got ready for bed and before she realized that she had gone to sleep, she was awakened to the sun glistening off of the fresh layer of snow that now covered everything, and to the sound of the tractor firing up. She just knew that her dad had slipped out in the early morning hours and fixed the tire and was starting the tractor, but to her surprise it was Mr. Gavin. He pulled the tractor in to the barn and left without any fan-fare.

CHAPTER 22

NO MORE CHURCH TALK

Oliver never slept past 5:30 in the morning, but this was no ordinary day. The previous day had been one for the record books. Though he wasn't hurting, he was extremely fatigued. He had rolled over to go back to sleep when he heard the door open, "Daddy, are you okay?" Asked Hazel. "He squinted and then rubbed his eyes, "Yes dear, I'm fine, just a little tired. What time is it?" "It's nearly 9:00, we've been in here a couple of times but you were sound asleep and we didn't want to bother you, but you never sleep this late so I thought I should make sure that you are okay," she said.

"Irene made you some grits for breakfast, do you want me to bring them to you?" "No, no, I need to get up anyway, I've got to get that tractor tire fixed," he replied. "Henry Gavin already fixed it, and he pulled it into the barn." She answered. "He did, and you let me sleep through it? Oh my, well," Oliver continued, "well, I guess I will have to run down to his place and let him know how grateful I am, but first, let's get us some grits. Why don't you bake some of that wheat bread and we'll take it down to him. I think there is some plum jam left, it's down in the," Hazel cut him off and said, "I already made him some and Irene went down in the cellar and got him some jam." "I suppose I can just go back to bed then," he laughed. "Come on daddy, Sister Irene has your breakfast ready." She responded.

Oliver stopped Hazel before she could say another word, "Now sweetheart, I don't want you to talk like that no more. I'm gonna tell Irene the same thing; I don't want anymore church talk. Those folks may be strange, but I think they mean well. We will just live our lives and let them live theirs. Is that fair enough?" He asked. "Fair enough daddy, but I didn't mean to make fun of them, I was just," This time he interrupted, "I know, let's just forget about it and go get some breakfast."

Hazel hadn't meant anything by her remarks, but she knew better than to say anymore. Oliver Trommel was never one to say much and she couldn't remember when he had spoken so emphatic about anything, so she thought it best to just let it go. She reached out her hand to help him up, but he just laughed at her. "Oh no you don't," He continued, "I may have had a spell, but I don't think I'm so bad that I should let my pregnant daughter be lifting on me. The last thing we need is for you to go into labor lifting on your old decrepit father!"

"Oh daddy, I'm not going into labor and your not old or decrepit." She said. Oliver rubbed his arm for a moment and then stood to walk with Hazel to the kitchen for breakfast. "Is your arm hurting daddy?" Hazel asked. "Oh it's nothing, I probably laid on it wrong, that's all." He replied. Oliver stopped for a moment and looked out the window at the snow that now covered the ground. "Oh my, we got quite a bit of snow didn't we?" He said. "Irene said that we got about three inches as best as she could tell." Hazel answered.

As they walked together into the living room Irene came rushing to Oliver's side to offer assistance. "Now stop that girls, I'm fine!" He stated emphatically. "You girls act like I'm half dead or something. I just had a little spell, it wasn't that bad!" He knew that it had been every bit as bad as they had thought and probably worse.

They walked with him to the kitchen table and sat down together for some grits and ham and a fresh pot of coffee. Knowing that Irene was about to start in on him, Oliver headed her off. "Now, Irene, I am fine and I would prefer to not discuss last night any further. Your sister here already has me in a home for the aged and feeble and I am fine." Oliver demanded. Hazel started to reply, but she knew that her dad was serious about the matter and thought it best just to leave it at that.

"Well, okay daddy, if that is what you want." Irene said. Oliver looked over her shoulder and out the window and said, "Well, it looks like we are in for some more snow." The girls turned to look, as the snow now began to fall in earnest. "Oh no, if it keeps this up, I don't know how I am going to make it home." Said Irene. "Well, don't get too far ahead of yourself honey, if I need to, I can drive you home and Robert can bring me back." Answered Oliver.

The snow continued for the better part of the morning. By the time that it had finally stopped and the skies started to clear, there was nearly seven inches of snow on the ground. "Well, it doesn't look like we are going to be going anywhere today." Said Oliver. "No, I'm afraid to drive in this much snow and you shouldn't be driving either daddy." Irene stated. "I told you, I'm fine and if I had anywhere to be today, I'd show you that..." Hazel cut Oliver off. "Daddy, Irene didn't mean anything by that, she is just looking out for your health, besides we don't have to go anywhere so we are all in luck."

They got the house straightened up and Irene and Hazel were busy putting away the dishes when they heard the back door close. Oliver had slipped out the back door and was heading toward the woodpile. Irene started toward the door, Hazel knew that she was going to try to stop Oliver from gathering fire wood and she caught her by the arm and said, "Irene, he isn't going to listen, so you might as well save your breath." They both stood there looking out of the window as they watched him sweep the snow off of the wood and gather up an armload of firewood.

"Is it just me, or does daddy seem a little grumpy?" Asked Irene. "No, it's not you, he has been a bear today. He griped at me a couple of times when I went in to tell him that breakfast was ready." Answered Hazel. "That's not like daddy to be like that, I mean, is it?" Irene asked. "No, I don't think I've ever had him yell at me or even raise his voice for that matter." She continued. "I know that he says he is fine, but I'm kind of worried about him." "Yeah me too." Replied Irene.

Oliver pushed the door open, "Whoa, it's cold out there!" He said. "Do you think we are going to get anymore snow daddy?" Irene asked. "No, I think it's over, at least for a while. Why don't we turn the radio on and see if they are saying anything about the weather?" Oliver said. Hazel walked across the room to the Philco radio and turned it on.

You could hear the tubes humming as it began to come alive. "This is Fibber McGee and Mollie inviting you to join us next time as Throckmorton P. Gildersleeve..." Hazel reached over and turned the station dial. "Hey, wait a minute, I wanted to hear that." Oliver said. "I thought you wanted me to check the weather?" Hazel asked. "Well, I did, but I would like to have heard what ole Gildersleeve is up to." Hazel hurried and turned it back, but it was too late.

They were advertising cigarettes and Oliver had missed hearing what he had wanted to hear, so he was none too happy. "Turn it to 840." Oliver said. Hazel quickly turned the dial to 840 am just in time as the announcer said, "This is News Radio 840 WHAS coming to you from the Churchill Downs, Eastern Kentucky is in for another round of snow this evening, it is expected to drop another three to five inches of snow over most of the region before coming to an end sometime early tomorrow morning."

Irene interrupted the rest of the news, clearly irritating her dad even more. "I've got to get home before I get snowed in." Without waiting for any replies from her dad or Hazel she rushed into the bedroom and gathered her things. "Irene, I'll take you home and Robert can get me back here before the snow hits." Said Oliver. "No daddy, I can't take a chance on you getting stuck, I'll be alright. I'll just take my time and drive carefully." Demanded Irene. She hurried to give her daddy a good-bye kiss and a hug and turned to Hazel and whispered, "Please keep and eye on him. Robert and I will be back over to check on him in a couple of days." She hugged her and rushed out the door nearly falling as she slid off of the bottom step.

The drive back to Salyersville was a very long one. The road was still covered with snow and although a few people had driven on it, it was extremely hazardous. She didn't like driving on this road alone when it was clear, let alone when it was covered in snow. The car was slipping and Irene was scared, if she was sliding on these straight stretches, how was she going to able to navigate Bromley pass. Bromley pass was a hill about seven miles south of Salyersville; it was the same place where she and Robert had a blowout. If you don't make that curve you are in trouble and she knew that it wasn't going to be a picnic, especially with the road conditions as they were.

Irene was sweating even though it was very cold out.

Suddenly she found herself praying, "Dear God, please help me get home! I can't do this by myself!" Suddenly she remembered that night that she and Robert had the blowout. She thought of how that she had chalked it up to luck, but somehow she now realized that it was not luck or happenstance that they got stopped before the tire blew. She remembered how Robert had said it was like he had heard a voice telling him to stop and when he did, the tire exploded. Suddenly Irene found herself thanking God for saving their lives that night. She knew that if that tire had blown while they were on Bromley pass, they would have both been killed.

"God, I know that I don't deserve it and I know that I owe you far more than I could ever pay you, but I'm asking for one more thing, please don't let me have a wreck." She prayed. As she approached the pass, it became harder to keep the car in the only set of tracks on the road.

The wind had blown the snow and there were places where you couldn't tell where the road stopped and the ditch started. Her hands were sweating profusely and she felt herself shaking. The rear end of the car slipped and she knew that she was in trouble. Irene struggled to steer into the slide, she was praying harder than she had ever prayed. She caught enough traction that the car straightened out, but her sense of relief was short lived.

Ahead of her she could see Bromley pass, the one set of tracks that had been her guide were now completely covered. There was nothing to guide her and without those tracks in the snow it was a guessing game.

Irene knew that if she didn't negotiate this curve, her life was over. She began to think of what would happen if she were to wreck and somehow live through it, how would anyone find her? Robert didn't know that she was coming home and her daddy wouldn't know that she hadn't made it. The more she thought about the "what if's" the more she became paralyzed by fear. Would she freeze to death before someone found her? Her car was again beginning to slip and she knew that the worst part of the road was right in front of her.

CHAPTER 23

STOP-DEATH-STOP

Matthew had not been himself since the last beating that he had experienced. He wasn't sure what was worse, the steady roar in his head, the damage to his mid-section, or extensive internal injuries from the gunshot to the abdomen. The regiment that lay in front of him was more than he could have handled before all of those injuries, let alone now. "The company" insisted that he run further and harder than he had ever run and the pressure was mounting with each assignment.

As much as he hated the thought of going through the local towns, he could now only wish that he was able to. Instead of running 30 to 100 miles and delivering moonshine, he was being sent into North Carolina and parts of Virginia. Most of the trips were in the middle of the night and the more he drove the more his head roared. He didn't know if it was from the lack of sleep or the bright lights of on-coming cars. All that he knew was, something had to give.

Matthew couldn't remember the last time that he had been home for more than a few hours at a time and although he was making plenty of money, he had long ago concluded that no amount of money was worth the head-aches that he was now experiencing. His, or rather, "the companies" car was a 1940 Ford v8 and it was as fast as it was good looking. Normally he would have thoroughly enjoyed driving such an incredible car, but not now. He actually dreaded the thought of getting in it.

The risk of getting caught hauling 'the merchandise' was too great to make the runs during the daylight hours. He had no idea what was in the car and to be truthful he didn't want to know. He never knew where they kept whatever it was, nor did he care.

Since the wreck, Matthew had done without a personal car altogether. Occasionally he had borrowed his dad's girlfriend's car, but that was over, now that his dad had developed cirrhosis of the liver. She left almost immediately after finding out about his sickness and with Matthew gone so much, there was no other option but to put his dad in a home for invalids.

It in that home that Matthew found his dad laying in a pool of blood where he had hemorrhaged to death.

The stress that he felt was overwhelming, and this trip was especially hard on Matthew. He was nearly nine hours from Inez, and no matter how hard he pushed the car, he knew that he would never make the deadline that was set for him. "What were they thinking, if I would have driven a steady 100 miles per hour the entire trip, I could never be back by 10:00 am." Matthew said aloud. He glanced at his watch and realized that was nearly 2:30 am. Although he was going more than 80 miles per hour, he pushed the peddle to the floor.

He was fuming as he thought about the predicament they had put him in. Why would they tell him to make a 20 hour trip and give him 14 to do it. Were they really that foolish? Being late was not an option; he wasn't sure what they might do to him if he didn't make it to Inez by 10:00. Whatever it was, it wouldn't be good. He was as near to having no option as he had ever been.

The engine in the Ford roared. He had topped 100 miles per hour and the speedometer was still climbing. Matthew began to replay all of his near misses and close calls. He thought of the wreck and the beating by Helen's dad. He thought about the gunshot and stomping that had completely destroyed him. He replayed the events of that day over and over in his mind. Faster and faster he sped down the winding road.

The 1940 ford was being pushed as hard as Matthew had ever pushed a car. At times he could feel it slip as he cut it hard into the curves, but he never let up on the gas. His mind was whirling, "Who was that guy? Why can't I see his face?" He seethed with anger and mumbled to himself. "If I ever find out who he was, I'll kill him!" Matthew screamed. Just then he remembered the truck. "That's it!" He shouted. "I know that truck." His mind raced as he replayed the moment that he had looked out of the window on the back door. He had caught a glimpse of the pickup truck that had been parked on the other side of the shed, but never thought anything of it, that is, until now.

It was the same truck the girl from Purdin had been sitting in when he met her for their date. That was the truck her old man had been sitting on, when they got back into town. "What was her name?" He muttered. "Hazel! That was her old man that shot me!" All of these months he had been trying to remember and now the whole scene began to play over in his mind.

There were no other cars on the road and it was a good thing. Matthew had thrown caution to the wind. He began to curse under his breath; his mind was going faster than the ford. He wasn't going to stop in Inez. He no longer cared about Clarence or the company, he no longer cared if he met their deadline or not. The only thing that he could think about was, how he was going to take care of Hazel's dad. He glanced at his watch; it was 4:43 am. If he kept this speed up, and he had every intention to do so, he could be in Purdin by 11:00. He was giving the Ford all that he had and was using every ounce of his energy steering into the curves, at times fighting to maintain control of the car. The road was narrow and the terrain was getting hillier. The curves were coming fast and furious! He began imagining the pleasure of getting even with... Suddenly, as he popped up over a hill at more than a hundred miles per hour, Matthew saw the lights flashing.

The sign that hang over the road was illuminated with neon lights and the words, "STOP – DEATH – STOP!" There was no time to stop! He tried! With every ounce of strength he had, Matthew was pushing down on the brake pedal.

CHAPTER 24

BAD TIMING

It was a blustery morning as Hazel accompanied her dad to town. She hadn't been out much since finding out that she was pregnant, primarily because of the shame that she felt and that she feared she had brought to her daddy. His name was impeccable and her foolishness had soiled that good name, at least that is the way that she saw it. She had seen the doctor a few times and although he had assured her that everything was progressing, as it should be. She had noticed a lot of swelling in her feet and ankles over the past couple of weeks, so she tried to stay off of her feet as much as possible.

Hazel also tried to stay as close to Oliver as possible, especially since his spell. She didn't know what else to call it but a spell. He hadn't said anything else about it and when she asked, he just shrugged his shoulders. She kept watching for signs or symptoms of ailments or illnesses, but there didn't seem to be any, still he had to follow up with Doctor Barton.

Hazel and Oliver arrived at the doctor's office a few minutes before Oliver's 9:30 am appointment and she noticed that he seemed a little distracted. "Daddy," she asked, "is everything okay? Are you hurting anywhere?" "No, no, sweetheart, I'm fine. I've just got a lot on my mind, but I'm just fine." "What is it daddy?" she continued, "Is there something that you want to talk about? We've got a few minutes to kill and I'm a pretty good listener." Oliver just stared out his window for a moment and then said, "No, I suppose I'm just a little sentimental that's all. It's just..." "Well good morning Oliver, how in the world are you?" Interrupted Dr. Barton who had walked up beside the truck. "Are you coming in or not?" He asked. "Oh good morning James, yes I'm coming in, you don't think I drove over here just to sit outside do you?" quipped Oliver.

Hazel was anxious to hear what it was that her dad was about to say but before she could ask anything else, he had opened the door and was getting out of the truck. "Wait daddy, what were you going to say?" she asked. Oliver looked back over his shoulder and replied, "We'll talk later." He closed his door and shook doctor Barton's hand and then came around to her side of the truck and opened the door and helped Hazel out. "You remember my daughter Hazel don't you James?" He asked. Doctor Barton reached out his hand to shake hers but as she reached for his hand she suddenly felt flushed, "Oh no, daddy, daddy, I think my water just broke." Hazel screamed. "Have you been having any pains or contractions?" Asked doctor Barton. Before Hazel could answer, she felt the most excruciating pain. "James, what do we need to do?" asked Oliver. "Let's get her inside, it looks like you are going to be a grandpa today Ollie. Little lady, are you ready to have this baby?" doctor Barton replied.

Before she had a chance to answer, another hard contraction hit her. Doctor Barton's assistant had noticed the commotion out front and had rushed out the front door to help get Hazel inside. Oliver felt helpless. He wished that his wife were here to help both of them understand what was going on and how to deal with it. Anna would know just what to say, she was such a confident person and always so calm, it was a trait that he wished that he had, but right now he felt anything but calm. If he could somehow get ahold of Irene, maybe she could help, but then again he thought, what would she be able to do, she had never had a child.

As he watched the assistant and doctor Barton working to get Hazel situated, Oliver felt a tinge in his left arm. At first he just shrugged it off, but then he remembered how he had felt the night that he was working on the tractor wheel. When he had reached for the wrench to break the lugs loose, he had this same sensation. Without saying anything, Oliver just sat down in the nearest chair that he could find. He was trying to take deep breaths to calm his heart rate. He didn't know what was going on, but he knew better than to take any chances.

He tried to distract himself with thoughts of the baby and how incredible it would be to have noise at the house, he thought about anything and everything, but still the discomfort in his arm continued. There was no way that he was going to interrupt the doctor, not when he was about to deliver his grand baby.

The assistant came around the corner and was about to ask Oliver a question when she noticed that he was ashen white and sweating profusely. "Are you alright sir?" she asked. Before Oliver could answer, she had turned and ran back into the room where Dr. Barton was working with Hazel. "Doctor, can I see you please?" she asked. "Well, Rose, I am quite busy at the moment in case you hadn't noticed." He remarked. "Yes sir, I know you are, but this is very important." she exclaimed. He could tell by her tone and by the look on her face that whatever it was, it could not wait.

When he got Hazel comfortable he stepped out into the hall where his assistant Rose was waiting. "This had better be good, Roseanna, or..." before he could finish she interrupted him, "Sir, something is wrong with Mr. Trommel. I didn't want to say anything in front of his daughter, but I think you need to come and take a look," she exclaimed. Doctor Barton hurried quickly to the lobby where Oliver was setting, he was very pail and his head was dripping with perspiration. "Ollie, are you alright? Are you nervous about being a grandpa?" he asked although he knew by the look on his old friends face that this was not about nerves.

Oliver's arm was hurting, but there was no way that he was going to make this day about himself, not when his daughter is in the other room about to deliver a baby. "No, I'm just fine James, I just need some air and maybe a drink of water," responded

Oliver. "Whoa, just a minute there old friend, lest you forget, I'm a doctor. I've seen this look a time or two and normally it happens pretty close to a funeral so don't play coy with me," returned doctor Barton. "I know that you are worried about your little girl, but the last thing that we need is you dying with a heart attack the same day that she gives birth to her baby, so I need you to listen to me and answer me straight, you got that?" he demanded. "Yes, I understand, but don't you think that you need to be in there with Hazel right now?" answered Oliver. "Oliver, is your chest hurting?" Are you having pains down your arm, your left arm? Do you feel short of breath?" Asked Dr. Barton.

"Doctor Barton, yes my arm is hurting, but I'm telling you, this is not the time to make a scene," answered Oliver. "Neither is a time to have you die here in my clinic!" Continued the doctor. "Now here is what we are going to do, I am going to get your daughter over to the hospital and she is going to have that baby, and I'm going to get you over to the hospital and you are going to rest and get checked out. We are going to find out what's going on with you. Now, we can do this my way or my way, is that clear Oliver Trommel?" Doctor Barton was in no mood to quibble with Oliver, he had just one thing more to say, "This is not up for discussion Ollie and I don't mean to be harsh, but I'm going to need you to get in the car with my assistant. She is going to drive you over to the hospital. You will wait there for Hazel and me. I want you to stay right with her and you have to promise me that if there is any change with you that you will tell her. Her name is Roseanna and she is pretty sharp so don't you try to fool her because she will know if you are lying to her." He continued. "I'm going to get Hazel into my car and take her over as well, if she asks us where you are I will tell her that you are already there and are waiting for us. I don't want her to see you looking like death. You follow me?"

With that, doctor Barton summoned his assistant and explained to her what he had in mind. Roseanna did as she was directed and hurriedly got Oliver into the car and over to the hospital. When they arrived at the hospital, Sister Anna Margaret who was the charge nurse at the hospital met Oliver. As soon as she was brought up to speed on what was happening at the clinic she rushed back inside to prepare the delivery room for Hazel. At the same time an attendant rushed out to Oliver's side with a wheel chair. "Let's get you inside sir." she said. By then, the pain in Oliver's arm had begun to subside and he was starting to feel somewhat normal. He attempted to persuade the attendant to let him walk in on his own accord, but she would have none of it. "Sir, I need you to have a seat!" She said emphatically. Oliver sat down and she rushed him straight into the emergency room.

Since her water broke, the pain had kept Hazel's attention away from her father and onto the baby that had decided to captivate her. Doctor Barton seemed to be on top of the situation and although the reason for them being at the clinic in the first place was her dad; she was glad that things turned out the way they did. Hazel was scared and wished that her mother were there with her. That was a wish that had been with her throughout her life, but now, especially now, how she wanted to have someone by her side who knew what to expect and could help her navigate these difficult waters.

Hazel wished there was some way to contact Irene, although Irene had never been anyone that she dreamed of sharing this moment with, the thought of being alone was more than Hazel could bear. The doctor had been out of the room for what seemed like forever. "Where could he have gone," Hazel thought aloud. The clinic was small, but the rooms were very clean and well kept and as she lay there between contractions trying to find something that she could focus her attention on, she noticed a picture of doctor Barton in his military uniform. There beside it were pictures of five children that she assumed were his, but where was his wife? There were no pictures of her, and that seemed odd to Hazel.

She knew that Dr. Barton had been good friends with both of her parents and based on the limited conversations that she had with her dad about Dr. Barton, she had deduced that he had even had a crush on her mom with they were kids. If it were under any other circumstances, she would perhaps ask him some questions about her mother. The memories of her mom had faded with time and although it may seem foolish to the doctor, Hazel would love to ask him what his mom was like when she was young? The diversion seemed to be working to some extent, but then another hard contraction hit. Hazel screamed in pain. The contraction was harder than the last one and lasted a little longer than it did.

As contraction let up, Hazel tried to get her mind on anything that may serve as a distraction. She couldn't help but wonder what had happened to Matthew, it seemed that he had dropped off of the face of the earth and that had been fine with her. Just thinking of him was enough to bring tears to her eyes. How could she have been so foolish and how could he have been so uncaring.

Hazel wondered if he even knew that she had gotten pregnant. It was probably best that he hadn't tried to contact her because she was pretty certain that her father would have welcomed him with his favorite shotgun. Still she had expected that he would have made an effort.

He had proved to be every bit the scoundrel that her sister had tried to warn her of. His reputation was actually much worse than she knew. Hazel couldn't help but wonder what she would tell her baby when it was old enough to ask questions, but she supposed there would be plenty of time to work on that. Another contraction hit, it nearly took her breath away. As it let up Hazel decided there was no use in wasting her thoughts on Matthew.

What was so important that the nurse took the doctor out of the room and what was taking them so long to do what ever it was they were doing? "Where is daddy?" Hazel asked out loud. "Why haven't they brought him back here with me?" There was no one in the room to answer her, so she yelled out, "Daddy, where are you?"

ABOUT THE AUTHOR

Dwight Jones is an author and also serves as Senior Pastor of Harvest Christian Centre (Assemblies of God) in Park Hills, Mo. He and Tammy, his wife of more than 30 years, have three daughters and four grandchildren. In addition to pastoring, he travels extensively preaching revivals and prophecy conferences as well as national and international conferences and camps.

For more information on the ministry of Pastor Dwight Jones, please visit him at reapnow.org or DwightJonesMinistries.com. You can also join people from more than 30 countries worldwide who watch the Reapnow broadcast on ROCU or on the web at reapnow.org.

For booking information or to contact Dwight, please call 573-760-2052

Made in the USA
Columbia, SC
08 March 2020